Shadow Catcher

*Also by Tim Champlin
in Large Print:*

Colt Lightning
Dakota Gold
Deadly Season
Flying Eagle
King of the Highbinders
The Last Campaign
Lincoln's Ransom
Summer of the Sioux
The Survivor
Swift Thunder
The Tombstone Conspiracy

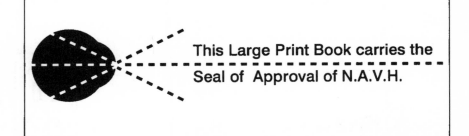

C013338602

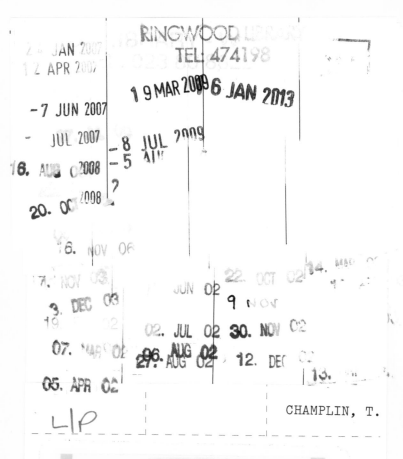

This book is due for return on or before the last date shown
above: it may, subject to the book not being reserved by
another reader, be renewed by personal application, post, or
telephone, quoting this date and details of the book.

Shadow Catcher

Tim Champlin

G.K. Hall & Co. • Waterville, Maine

Copyright © 1985 by Tim Champlin

Published in 2001 by arrangement with Golden West Literary Agency.

G.K. Hall Large Print Western Series.

The text of this Large Print edition is unabridged.
Other aspects of the book may vary from the original edition.

Set in 16 pt. Plantin by Al Chase.

Printed in the United States on permanent paper.

Library of Congress Cataloging-in-Publication Data
Champlin, Tim, 1937–
    Shadow catcher / Tim Champlin.
      p.   cm.
    ISBN 0-7838-9494-5 (lg. print : hc : alk. paper)
    1. Photographers — Fiction. 2. Arizona — Fiction. 3. Large
type books. I. Title.
PS3553.H265 S52 2001
813′.54—dc21   2001024441

For my good friend, Ken Donnelly,
the "Tall Tennessean"

Chapter 1

The golden warmth of the midday Arizona sun was lulling me into a doze when the crack of a rifle shot brought me straight up in my saddle. Two more shots followed in quick succession. The boom of the heavy-caliber rifles resounded through the still air.

"Where is it?" Wiley Jenkins asked as we both reined up and I reached instinctively for the new Winchester '73 carbine in the scabbard of my McClellan saddle. My eyes swept the brown desert hills ahead, but I saw no movement, no smoke, nothing. The silence settled in once more as if the balmy autumn day had not been disturbed.

"I knew we should have come into the territory by one of the passes a few miles north," Wiley said grimly, as he squinted from under his hat brim at the empty stage road that wound ahead into Apache Pass. "But there's no water up that way. So it's either take a chance on the Apaches or . . ."

Two more shots cut off the sound of his words and we checked our horses quickly as they started.

"Sounds like they're just out of sight around that next bend."

"Those shots sound like they might be coming from army Springfields. Fort Bowie's around here somewhere. Could be the troops are taking a little routine target practice," I remarked, more to calm my pounding heart than to convince Wiley.

"Never knew the army to issue extra ammunition for that purpose."

We sat our horses for an uneasy moment or two.

"Well, shall we take a look?" Wiley glanced across at me. The only arm he carried was a long-barreled Colt .45. Although he was dead set against violence in general, and war in particular, it had taken no persuasion to get him to carry a sidearm into the country of the notorious Apache. "From my earlier experience in the Arizona Territory, any fighting against the Apache is going to be done at close range or not at all," had been his comment a month ago as he selected the beautiful ivory-handled, nickel-plated weapon in a Deadwood gunshop. "If they're beyond the range of this, I'll be running, not fighting."

But just now he sat his horse a few feet to my right, his gun still holstered. "Well?" he asked again, a little impatiently.

I nodded. "Okay. But take it easy. No tellin' what we may be riding into. Too bad there's no way we could circle around and come up on that firing, easy like."

"I'm sure those shots came from that direction." Wiley pointed to his right.

I eased down the hammer of my Winchester and kneed my horse forward at a walk. Wiley did the same, as we moved off the stage road and began a gradual climb between two hills. There were no more gunshots, and the clopping of our horses' hooves on the hard ground seemed unusually loud. The rounded, rock- and mesquite-covered hills began to enfold us like the smothering arms of death. My chest felt tight and I had difficulty breathing.

We rode almost a mile with nothing but the desert stillness, and wound ourselves deep into the pass. Wiley had told me that even though he had never seen it, Fort Bowie was supposed to be in or very close to Apache Pass. There was no sign of it so far.

A sudden fusillade crashed so loudly I thought someone was shooting at us. I slid off my horse, rifle in one hand and reins in the other. We quickly led our horses off to the left and I looked up at the rocky, brush- and cactus-covered hills that rose all around us. Still nothing. Three more shots reverberated off the rocks.

"That sounded more like a handgun," I said, still searching the slopes for some sign of the shooters. There were few trees or rocks large enough to hide both our horses and us, but in the draw stood a palo verde tree. Wiley followed my lead as I tied my dun securely to one of its branches.

"I think it's coming from just beyond this

hill," Wiley whispered. "Think we can climb up and get a look from above?"

"Let's give it a try."

The hill was not over a hundred feet high, but it was fairly steep. As we began to climb, I regretted not having a sling for my carbine, which would leave my hands free. We slipped and slid and clawed our way up the pitched slope, pausing a couple of times to listen for any further sounds of fighting. My own ragged breathing and pounding heart were the only sounds I heard.

We finally reached the crest of the hill and crawled forward carefully. We had to move about twenty yards before reaching a point where the hill began to drop away enough for us to see over the other side. At first I saw nothing at all, but as we edged farther, wriggling forward among some scrub mesquite and prickly pear, I spotted a wagon near the base of the hill below us. A team of mules was harnessed to it, but no one was on the driver's seat.

"That's an army ambulance!" Wiley whispered to me.

"I don't think so," I replied, narrowing my eyes to read the lettering on the side of the tall, enclosed wagon box. The wagon stood at an angle to me, but I could still make out the large white letters on the dark green background. "At least it's not an army ambulance anymore," I whispered. "That says, PADDY BURKE — PHOTOGRAPHER. Looks like a converted ambulance, all right."

Suddenly, a puff of smoke burst from the front of the wagon as a rifle cracked at some unseen target in the hills to my left. The mules jumped at the sudden noise. It was then I noticed their reins trailing on the ground. An answering burst of gunfire kicked up dust around the wagon and I heard a bullet whine off the rocks beyond. The edgy mules jumped again and began sidling away, pulling the wagon around toward us. Just then a half-dozen mounted Apaches whipped their horses into view from behind an outcropping to the left and rode toward the ambulance, firing as they came. While they were still a good thirty or forty yards from the wagon, Wiley and I cut loose at them. Firing downhill, we had a tendency to shoot high, but by some lucky shot, one of us hit a pony who stumbled and pitched his rider off. While two of the raiders kept up a covering fire at the front of the wagon, the three remaining Apaches rode up and began cutting the mules out of their traces. The warrior who had been thrown was yelling and pointing toward us on the hillcrest where the smoke from our muzzles had betrayed our prone positions.

The two who had been covering the wagon swung their repeaters at us and cracked off a couple of shots. Although they were firing from horseback, a slug kicked up dirt about three feet in front of my face. I rolled to the left, the rocky soil digging into my stomach and arms, and threw the lever on my Winchester. I fired twice

11

more, quickly, but was still shooting high. Suddenly one of the Apaches jerked, arching his back, and fell from his horse. A shot from inside the wagon hit him. The nearest raider leaped from his horse onto the seat of the wagon and plunged inside, while the three remaining horsemen turned their fire on us once more.

As I ducked back from the fusillade, I caught a glimpse of the one Indian whose horse had been shot. He was between the plunging mules, slashing at their leather harness. As the firing slackened, I eased my head back up and took careful aim, lowering the muzzle slightly, and squeezed off a shot. The rifle went spinning out of the hands of one of the riders, and he grabbed his wrist. Just then, the riderless warrior finally freed the mule team and leaped onto the back of one of the animals. With a yell, he waved at the others and, leading the three other mules, kicked his mount. The remaining Apaches plunged away, their long black hair flying. They had their plunder, but it had cost them one wounded and possibly one dead, along with the loss of one horse.

One Indian was still inside, and the wagon was rocking with evidence of struggle. A muffled shot came from inside the wagon and the Apache tumbled limply out the rear doors into the dust.

A shot exploded next to me as Wiley fired his Colt, and I saw the three Apaches swing back toward us. While two of them returned our fire, the third slid off his horse and retrieved the body of the fallen tribesman. We flattened out, but their hurried, uphill shooting was ineffective. When I raised my head again, it was to the sound of hoofbeats. The war party was leaving!

Wiley and I jumped up, bounded over the crest of the hill, and began running and plunging down the steep hillside, sliding in the loose rocks and dirt, and dodging the spiny yucca plants along the way. As we finally reached level ground and approached it, there was no sign of life from the deserted wagon. My heart was pounding and my breath came in gasps from the sudden exertion. It was ominously quiet. Holding my rifle at hip level, I motioned for Wiley to approach the rear while I approached the front. A rifle barrel slid around the edge of the bullet-scarred wood.

"Hello, the wagon!" I yelled hurriedly.

A flushed face topped by disheveled auburn hair appeared.

"Have those red devils gone? Rats! I wanted to get my hands around the windpipe of another of those thievin', stinkin' savages. One got in here and knifed my apprentice, but he won't be cuttin' anybody else — unless he picks a fight in the happy huntin' grounds." His blood was still up and his blue eyes blazed. He was panting from the struggle and there was a fresh abrasion on one cheekbone. Sweat dripped from his nose.

As he talked he was reaching down a hand to help me up onto the wagon seat. He wiped a

13

sleeve across his perspiring face. "Where did you two come from? Well, wherever it was, you couldn't have arrived at a better time," he continued, without waiting for an answer. "I thought there were a lot of shots coming from someplace besides my rifle and those Indians. Sure is good to see a friendly face," he said, pumping my hand. "Paddy Burke's the name, I'm a photographer out of New York City," he said quickly. "God! I've got to see about Chris." He dove back into the wagon where Wiley already had the boy propped up on the floor, ripping away parts of his bloody shirt.

With the light flooding in from both ends, I could see that the interior of the tall, converted ambulance was lined with shelves containing rows of bottles and jugs of clear and smoked glass and stoneware, some with labels and some without. There was a long, narrow worktable down one side. One of the shelves had been broken loose in the struggles, and the shattered bottles on the floor had loosed a strong chemical odor, like some kind of acid. In fact, the smell was so overpowering that Wiley motioned for me to help him get the pale youth up and outside. With the clutter and the broken glass on the floor, there was no room for the wounded boy to lie down. He moaned softly as we half carried, half dragged him out the rear doors and gently put him down in the shade of the ambulance. Wiley had bared the chest of the lanky youth and, with a piece of the torn shirt, was at-

14

tempting to staunch the flow of blood from a wound in the left shoulder. There was so much blood that I couldn't see the extent or nature of the wound, but I feared the worst. However, when I got a closer look, I saw that the injury to the upper left chest was more of a slash than a stab. But it was several inches long and he was losing a lot of blood. As soon as Wiley formed a compress of the torn shirt and pressed it on the cut, the boy passed out in a dead faint.

I glanced up at the grim man standing above me. He was still breathing hard from his struggle, and rivulets of perspiration were running down his face. He was on the low side of medium height and build, but appeared wiry and strong with a whiplike strength. His hair was a wavy dark auburn and his eyes were blue. I turned my attention back to Wiley and the boy.

"What do you think?"

"If we can get this bleeding stopped, I think he's got a chance. Can't tell if anything vital was cut."

"I've got some alcohol in the wagon if you need it," the red-haired man behind me said.

"Okay, but we'll need to get this bleeding stopped, and then we can worry about disinfectant."

"You're not a doctor, are you?" the man asked.

"No." Wiley answered over his shoulder. "Just seems like I've run into a lot of wounds in the last few years. I've had a lot of unwanted practice.

You could fetch the alcohol, though."

The man was back in a few seconds with a bottle and a clean cotton cloth, and began swabbing the drying blood off his apprentice's chest while Wiley held the compress firmly in place.

"This boy needs better medical attention than I can give him," Wiley said after a few minutes. "D'ya reckon there's a doctor at Fort Bowie?"

"Don't know," the man replied. "We were headed there when these Indians jumped us. Damn! I would've thought they'd be afraid to attack this close to the garrison."

"If they had any patrol out, I'm surprised they didn't hear the shots," I remarked. "We must have been a good mile from here, and we heard 'em loud and clear. Wonder how far the fort is from here?"

"I don't know," the man answered. "We were just hoping we'd hit it before dark."

I started to ask him what he was doing in Apache country, but thought better of it. Besides, he could have been wondering the same about us. The various Apache tribes had been stubbornly resisting the incursion of whites for more than a generation. And they'd had a lot of practice on the Mexicans and Spanish for two hundred years before that. They had successfully harassed travelers and settlers since the first whites were foolhardy enough to pursue mineral wealth in this part of the country. They had not prevented the Butterfield stage line from running through Apache Pass, nor the establishment of Fort Bowie. But the Butterfield Line had ceased to operate some fifteen years before, in 1862, even though the small fort was still there.

"Even if we knew where it was or how far, I don't think this boy should be moved tonight," Wiley said.

"I could ride for the fort and bring somebody back here," I volunteered. "Maybe if we're in luck, they'll have a surgeon assigned to the post."

"I wouldn't be riding anywhere in this pass alone," the redheaded man said. I was inclined to agree with his advice.

"Here, elevate his feet," Wiley said. The man reached into the wagon for a small wooden box and placed it under the boy's boots.

I stood there watching Wiley work on the apprentice as he pressed on the compress with one hand and felt for the boy's pulse with the other. "I don't think that Apache's knife penetrated the chest wall, so there shouldn't be any internal bleeding," he remarked almost to himself. "But it slashed hell out of the muscles — maybe cut a small artery." The boy's eyes were still closed, and his face was pale.

"His pulse is strong and steady. If we keep him right still until this bleeding stops, I think he'll pull through. It's pretty chancy, though. We'll need to get some medical help."

"I'd better go bring the horses around," I said after another minute or so. "Whether I ride for the fort or not, we'll need 'em to pull this wagon out of here."

"We can't move this boy tonight," Wiley repeated firmly. "We'll have to camp here and see how he is in the morning."

The afternoon shadows were stretching longer and the warmth of the October sun was waning as evening came on. It was going to be a cold night. I picked up my rifle and started off to retrieve our horses.

"Hey, mister."

I stopped.

"Thanks." Paddy Burke stuck out his hand. I shifted my Winchester to my left hand and gripped his. His grip was strong.

"That's my apprentice, Christopher Barnwell." He jerked his head in the direction of the unconscious boy. "We owe you two our lives. I won't forget it." In turn, I formally introduced myself, Matt Tierney.

As I looked into his steady blue eyes, I instinctively liked this man. He was either uncommonly cool in the face of hostile Apaches, or else he had his nerves under a tight rein. From what I had heard of the fighting abilities of Apache warriors, killing or disabling one of them in hand-to-hand combat was no mean feat.

I heard the hoofbeats just a second or two before a rifle cracked. Dust spurted near a front wagon wheel.

Burke jumped for his rifle, which he had leaned against the wagon, and I dove under-

18

neath, levering a shell into the chamber of my rifle. The Apaches were back! I snapped off a shot and saw one of the galloping horses rear, squealing, almost throwing its rider. There were several warriors; whether or not they were the same ones as before, I couldn't tell. Caught in the open with a severely wounded boy, I cursed myself for not going for our horses immediately. Bad judgment in such a dangerous situation could prove fatal.

Chapter 2

I rolled over and fumbled frantically for the cartridges in my belt loops. Fortunately, Wiley's Colt was exploding nearby, and I was aware of Burke's Henry cracking off shots to my left.

"They've already got my mules. What else d'the murderin' savages want?" Burke yelled above the noise, squeezing off a shot through the dust as the half-dozen horsemen swerved in toward the wagon.

An arrow whanged off an iron wheel rim and grazed my cheek. Well, at least they weren't *all* armed with rifles, I thought as I thumbed the last of the handful of shells into the loading gate of my Winchester. But before I could even get off another shot, the raiders had veered away under the steady fire of Burke and Wiley Jenkins.

The pony that had been hit stumbled and fell, while its rider, kicking free and rolling to his feet, was swept up behind one of the other Apaches. The attackers drew their ponies up out of effective range, partially hidden by the slope of an alluvial dry wash. The wounded pony lay kicking in the middle distance. Just as I noticed him, a shot from Burke's rifle crashed next to my ear and the animal dropped its head suddenly.

"I'm not for seein' the poor beast suffer," he

remarked as I twisted around to look at him.

"What're they up to?" I asked Wiley as we eyed the Indians who were sitting their horses and moving slowly around on the uneven desert floor in the distance.

"Not sure. Only had one other brush with Apaches, and that was with a bunch of Warm Springs warriors a few years back," Wiley answered.

"Are those the same ones who attacked you a few minutes ago?" I asked Burke over my shoulder, from where I still lay on my belly under the wagon.

"I didn't get a real good look, but I think it was," he replied slowly.

I rolled out from under the ambulance and looked around for some better shelter. But there didn't seem to be anything close. The slope at the base of the hill that we had just descended was only a few rods away, but we'd never be able to climb it fast enough if the Indians decided to charge, especially since we had a severely wounded boy on our hands, and any jostling of him would certainly reopen his knife wound. No, our best chance for the moment seemed to be to stay by the wagon. The open desert terrain offered no shelter except for some mesquite and small barrel cactus. The hills around us offered a few bare rock outcroppings near their summits, possibly large enough to shelter us, but they were out of reach. The sides of the converted ambulance were not thick enough to stop a bullet, so there seemed no point in climbing back inside for protection. Besides, I for one wanted a clear view of the danger that confronted us.

"Anything in that wagon they might be after?" I asked Burke, taking advantage of the lull to finish loading my rifle.

"Not that I know of, unless they want a couple of cameras, some glass plates and some chemicals."

"Can you think of any reason they'd be attacking you again?"

He ran a sleeve across his still-perspiring face. "No. They already got my mules. I haven't been in this country long enough to know what Apaches consider valuable."

"They probably want revenge for your killing one of their warriors," Wiley said, looking toward the barely visible cluster of riders in the distance. "Apaches don't take kindly to that kind of thing. They got your mules, all right, but they want to punish you now. Maybe have your ears decorate a breech clout — after they've staked you out in the sun to dry for a day or two and let their women carve you up."

A chill went up my back at these words and I glanced at the photographer. His red face seemed to go a couple of shades lighter. But then he gripped his Henry rifle tighter and stepped up to the corner of the wagon. "Then, by God, let 'em come, I'll show 'em what a hard-nosed Yankee Irishman can do in a fight! I've never done a damn thing to them, except stop at the San Carlos agency and take a few views of them. And even then I gave most of my pictures to them in return for the favor."

"Not very likely these are any of the same Indians," Wiley said, rising from his kneeling position on the ground beside the still-unconscious apprentice. "I hear Victorio and a bunch of his followers have jumped the reservation and are raiding over the whole southern part of the territory and into Mexico."

"Did you do anything to get 'em riled up while you were over at San Carlos?" I asked.

"No," Burke answered, a trace of irritation in his voice. "I went through the agent, John Clum, and got permission, and also talked to a few of the minor chiefs. Most of them were delighted with their pictures. They were the envy of their friends." He paused thoughtfully. "The Utes up in Colorado were the only ones who were really opposed to my making any views of them. They thought my camera was some kind of a strange box of bad medicine. Called me the 'shadow catcher.' 'Make Indian heap sick,' they told me. 'Squaw die, papoose die, pony die, all die,' they said. And they just plain refused to come near me. Even some of the Sioux thought they would die in three days if I took their photographs." In spite of our perilous situation, he almost smiled at the recollection. "Their medicine men had them convinced I was stealing their spirits."

"Well, we're fixin' to find out if this bunch can

steal our spirits," Wiley said, indicating the riders coming up out of the wash several hundred yards distant.

A sharp whistle sounded behind us. I spun around, rifle ready, thinking the Apaches had somehow gotten behind us while diverting our attention. I knew that whistle came from no bird I had ever heard. But I saw nothing. The desert hills appeared empty. Then the shrill whistle split the air again, and I spotted a man waving his arms, motioning for us to come toward him. His faded clothing had blended so well into the dun-colored desert terrain behind him that I had not been able to pick him out at first.

"Hurry! Hurry!" he yelled. "It's your only chance!"

I glanced back toward the hostiles, and my heart skipped a beat as I saw the horsemen riding out of the wash at a gallop and heading toward us.

"Here they come again!" Wiley yelled at the same time. "And they aren't lookin' to parley."

Even from a distance of a quarter-mile, the Apaches looked fearsome, their long black hair flying and the late-afternoon sun glinting from their weapons. Their high-pitched yells carried to us over the low rumble of their ponies' hooves.

"Let's go!" Burke said, thrusting his rifle at Wiley and scooping up his slim apprentice in one quick motion. "I don't know who that man is, but we need all the help we can get right now!"

With the strength born of fear, he started to run with the half-conscious boy in his arms. Wiley shoved his Colt into his belt and, with one quick glance in the direction of the onrushing Indians, hefted the Henry in one hand and began his retreat with us. The ground was uneven and studded with small rocks and shrubs and cactus, and we stumbled in our haste. But the amazing Burke almost hounded over the rough terrain, carrying the injured youth.

As we neared the man who had yelled at us, he swung his aim and pointed, "this way," and he quickly disappeared around a sharp rock outcropping on the side of the hill. He was gone so quickly, that I had the feeling he was a bearded apparition that did not really exist — a human mirage. But I threw a quick glance over my shoulder and knew that those mounted Apaches were no mirage. They had seen us retreating from the cover of the wagon and were yelling in triumph, realizing they had us trapped in the open. They had almost reached the wagon. I saw all of this in the quick second before I jumped behind the outcropping. A rifle cracked behind me at the same instant that a bullet spanged off the rock I had just vacated.

About forty feet ahead and slightly below me was a square black opening in the face of the hill. My companions were slipping and sliding diagonally across the loose shale in their haste to reach it. We probably had less than half a minute, I guessed, before the raiders rounded the base of the hill and got us in point-blank range.

I caught up with Wiley just as he was relieving the winded Burke of his burden. Chris, the apprentice, was unconscious again, and the photographer's shirt front was smeared with blood from the boy's wound. Between Wiley and myself, we half dragged the boy to the mouth of the crudely timbered mine shaft.

I was so intent on getting to cover that I didn't hear the Apaches until a whoop behind me and the sound of two shots sent me sprawling on my belly the last few feet into the opening. I was the last one in as someone grabbed the back of my belt and finished pulling me inside. The Henry was erupting in smoke and flame over my head as Wiley countered the attack. Even though the rifle barrel was outside, the explosions were deafening in the confined space. I suddenly remembered my own rifle and was surprised to find it still clutched tightly in my right hand as I crawled on my hands and knees along the floor of the tunnel. With a quick tug or two on the collar of the wounded boy, I pulled him back into the shaft a few feet out of the way and then jumped to the aid of Wiley who was still working the lever of Burke's old Henry rifle. I flattened myself against the rough wall of the tunnel opposite Wiley and laid the gun barrel around the timber that framed the opening.

With both of us laying down a withering fire from this cover, the Apaches quickly saw the futility of further pursuit and kicked the sides of their ponies in a fast retreat. As near as I could tell, our hasty fire had not been deadly, effective only in driving them off. If we had hit either horses or riders, it wasn't evident as they galloped off in the swirling dust. But I was still panting so hard that I couldn't have drawn a bead on any target, especially a moving one. I was firing fast, but emptied my Winchester in the direction of the fleeing Indians to no effect.

"Whew! Thank God!" Wiley breathed, stepping back and leaning the empty Henry against the wall beside him. I automatically put my rifle on half-cock safety and did the same. But this time I began slipping cartridges out of my belt loops to reload. I had learned my lesson about leaving my weapon empty, although I didn't think the Apaches would return soon.

"Besides thanking God, we should be thanking this gentleman, here," Burke said, indicating the man who had rescued us. I looked back at the man who was standing silently about twenty feet behind us in the deepening gloom of the old mine tunnel. After looking outside, my eyes took a few seconds to adjust to the dimness. The man who finally came into focus was about six feet tall and heavily bearded with hair that was almost shoulder length. The faded canvas pants were held up by wide galluses, and the pale blue shirt was stained darker across the chest and under the arms by sweat. The miner's boots had seen some hard usage as had his hat, a high-crowned black felt similar to those worn by

Union soldiers during the war. The wide brim was pinned up on one side, giving the man a rakish look, belied by the rest of his appearance. The overall impression I got was that of a miner down on his luck.

"Where, in God's name, did you come from, man?" Burke addressed the silent specter. "First I'm saved by these men, and then all of us are rescued by you. I've been twice blessed today. Paddy Burke's the name, an itinerant photographer." He stepped forward and offered his hand. The man ignored the handshake, brushed past Burke with a lumbering gait, and thrust his head out of the tunnel entrance. Then he took a few steps outside and looked intently off to the west where the sun was low on the jagged horizon. After a minute or two he came back inside.

"I don't think those Apaches will be back, at least not today," he said in perfectly clear, precise English. "If they'd had something with them to light it, they'd have fired your wagon, just for spite," he continued, "after stripping off anything usable."

It was a shock to hear him speak. I don't know exactly what I had expected, but I think I was waiting for him to talk like he looked — uncouth and uncultured.

As I looked at this man, I sensed something odd about him. He appeared to have been a big, robust, heavily muscled man at one time. Or at least his bone structure indicated it. But now he was lean and stoop-shouldered — almost had a wasted appearance, like someone who had been in the throes of a long illness. Even his face — what I could see of it behind the tangle of hair and beard — looked pale, like that of a man who spends all his time indoors or underground. Of course, if he were a miner, that could account for his paleness in this land of nearly perpetual sunshine. And hard physical labor might account for his leanness. But it was not a hard-muscled leanness. Maybe he had come to this country because of poor health — but surely not to unsettled Apache country! It took only a few seconds for these things to run through my mind. If I could grip his hand, I could tell if he was accustomed to hard labor. But he showed no inclination to shake hands.

While I was sizing up our benefactor and slipping the last of my belted cartridges into my rifle, Burke and Wiley were kneeling beside the apprentice, tending his oozing wound.

"What about our horses?" Wiley said suddenly, straightening up. "I hope those Apaches didn't find them or we're in real trouble. A man without a horse in this country might as well be without water."

"Where did you leave them?" the bearded one asked.

"Back on the other side of this hill," Wiley replied.

"They should be safe, then," the man answered evenly, showing no trace of excitement or emotion. "That raiding party rode off to the southwest — probably back toward the Chiracahuas or the Dragoons."

"I'll go after the horses," I offered. "You stay with that boy and do what you can," I said to Wiley. Chris was conscious but still flat on his back.

"I'm coming with you," Burke said, retrieving his Henry and pushing the lever part way open to see if a shell was in the chamber. Then he jacked the lever all the way open. It was empty. He fished in the leather pocket of his vest. "Ah, four shells left. The rest are in the wagon." He shoved the .44 rim-fire cartridges into the rifle, and with a last look at the deathly pale apprentice and the strange man who had rescued us, he cautiously started out after me.

"Rats!"

"What's wrong?" Startled, I glanced back at Burke as we dug the edges of our boots into the steep hillside, climbing up and away from the black mouth of the tunnel.

"We were just about making expenses these last three weeks. The loss of those mules, plus the wounding of my apprentice, will just about put me out of business altogether."

He was silent for a few moments as we continued climbing.

"Maybe if I can salvage my wagon and whatever isn't broken inside it, I may be able to sell it. Might be able to find another photographer in Tucson who will buy the whole rig — provided I can find some way to *get* it to Tucson . . ." His voice trailed off as our climbing became more arduous and our breathing heavier. "Could swap . . . the wagon for a horse and pack mule . . . keep one small camera and just enough plates, collodian, and hypo . . . maybe keep on awhile longer . . ."

I didn't reply to his mullings since by this time I was panting myself.

We finally reached the summit of the hill near the spot where Wiley and I had first opened fire on the war party. We paused to look around. Showing ourselves like that against the skyline would ordinarily have been a very careless, possibly fatal, thing to do. But there was no question about any Apaches knowing we were in the vicinity, plus the fact that we feared no hostile long-range sharpshooter among the Indians.

Burke's bullet-riddled converted spring ambulance still rested forlornly at the base of the hill, its white lettering catching the last rays of the westering sun. The photographer looked down at it with the expression of a man who has just lost most of his worldly possessions.

"Well, at least they didn't burn it," I consoled him. "You can fix it up and replace the mules."

"Not without money," he replied. "But I'll manage somehow." He smiled grimly. "I never expected this would be like running a portrait business in New York City. I've had my share of problems since I finished working on the Hayden Geological Expedition last year. And I've managed to make it so far."

31

We plunged on down the other side of the hill to where our horses were still securely tied, tugging impatiently at their reins. It seemed like a long time since we had left them, but in fact it had only been about a half hour. Out here, the only clocks were the sun and stars although the towns, railroads, and the military attempted to keep some sort of local time. The railroads alone had over seventy different times in the country.

It felt good to swing up into the saddle again. Burke mounted Wiley Jenkins's horse and we rode warily around the base of the hill toward his wagon to pick up the rest of his ammunition and any food he might have.

"We've been down to crackers and coffee for three days," he replied when I questioned him about his supplies. Wiley and I carried only the barest of staples in our saddlebags.

As we rode with our rifles across our pommels, our eyes continuously scanned the hilltops around us, even though I knew it was a futile exercise. If we were to be ambushed again, we would never see the Indians until they fired or were upon us. Many a traveler by horse, coach, and wagon had been waylaid in Apache Pass during the last thirty years. The various Apache tribes might have had just cause at one time, but still I didn't want to become another victim of their vengeance. During our journey from Chicago, Wiley had regaled me with horror stories about the Apaches' favorite ways of dispatching enemy captives. Being flayed alive, being hung naked over a cliff by one leg, being staked out in the sun and blinded by a burning stick, or being the victim of any other fiendish torture was not the way I wanted to end up my first foray into the Arizona Territory. Maybe Wiley and I should have stayed in the safer areas of the territory. But safety was not the reason we came to Arizona. News of the recent mineral discoveries was coming out of the southern part of the territory. And besides, wasn't Camp Bowie near here? The attack on Burke had proved there was no real safety even with troops fairly close.

"I'm surprised a patrol from Camp Bowie didn't ride out to see what all the commotion was about," I commented aloud.

"You'd think somebody from the fort would have heard it," the photographer agreed.

We came up to his wagon without seeing anyone at all.

"It's only about a hundred yards around the base of the hill to the mouth of the tunnel," I said. "Want to try pulling it closer?"

There was little left of the slashed harness, but we were able to piece together enough of the leather straps with ropes from the wagon to fasten one long piece from each of our saddles to either side of the wagon tongue. In this manner we managed to drag the wagon awkwardly most of the distance to the point where the hill began to slope upward about twenty yards from the mouth of the tunnel. At least here it would be within sight and effective pistol range of the tunnel, where we intended to spend the night.

As we dismounted and untied the makeshift harness, our mysterious benefactor led a saddled mule out of the tunnel. The mine must be a lot deeper than I first suspected, if the mule had been inside all the time; I had seen no sign of the animal earlier.

Without a word to anyone, the man pulled himself up onto the mule and prepared to ride off.

"Hey, which way to Camp Bowie?" I yelled to him, feeling I had to say something to detain him. I couldn't believe the man was leaving so quickly. There were too many questions we needed to ask him. We hadn't even had a chance to thank him. Wiley appeared in the tunnel entrance, when he heard my voice. I glanced questioningly at him and he shrugged and shook his head.

The man pointed in a general southeast direction. "About two miles as the buzzard flies," he said, and then kicked his mule in the sides and trotted off down to the desert floor, past the wagon, and headed west, ignoring our shouts. No offer of further help, no attempt at friendship, nothing.

The sun was down, but the entire western sky was ablaze with streaks of red and gold — a glorious splash of color that threw a slightly brighter afterglow over our small group on the hillside.

Burke joined me in staring after the back of the retreating rider in the desert dusk.

"Friendly cuss, isn't he?"

"Maybe he's on the run himself."

"Could be. He looked pretty rough — like he'd been hiding out."

"Whoever he is, we owe him our lives," Wiley added, coming up to where we stood. The figure of the mule and rider had vanished into the gathering gloom, and the sounds of his hoofbeats faded, leaving the hush of twilight.

There was no thought of trying to find Camp Bowie in the unfamiliar terrain, especially with Apaches in the area. From what Wiley had told me, we were in less danger from attack at night than during daylight. But Apaches were also well known for their inurement to discomfort and pain, their patience, and their ability to move about in their native territory unseen and unheard. They had been known to walk and run fifty miles in a day on very little food and water and still have the strength to fight at the end of it.

While we were gone, Chris had become semi-conscious, and Wiley used the remainder of the boy's shirt to staunch the reopened knife wound.

"The boy's going into shock," Wiley said. "If we can find some dead brush to get a fire going and make some coffee right quick, maybe we can counteract it. He needs some hot stimulant. Otherwise . . ." He didn't finish, but we all knew the youth might not see another sunrise. He had lost a lot of blood. Wiley grabbed the blanket from Burke and formed a pad under the boy's back, then unrolled a blanket from behind his

35

own saddle to cover the boy where he lay, a few feet inside the tunnel. Then he began massaging the youth's hands and feet.

Being careful not to stray too far from the mine, I quickly gathered some sticks and dead brush. Forming a small pile near the entrance, I tore a page from the notebook I carried in my shirt pocket and crumbled it up under the wood. Then I struck a lucifer and, carefully feeding twigs to the tiny blaze, managed to get a small cooking fire going.

While I was at this, Burke had taken a handful of coffee beans, dropped them into a buckskin bag, and was pounding them with a rock. It wasn't long before the water was heating in the smoke-blackened coffee pot, which we had balanced on two flat rocks. There was no shortage of water. Wiley and I had more than a quart left in each of our canteens. A stray bullet had penetrated the five-gallon water barrel in the ambulance, but fortunately had struck about halfway up, leaving a good two gallons.

There was nothing to cook, and not much to say, so the three of us silently passed around the beef jerky and cheese and crackers. We had built the small fire just outside to keep any smoke out of the protective tunnel, but we all sat back out of the firelight or stayed inside the cover of the hillside. I don't know if Burke and Wiley Jenkins felt it, but as I sat with my back against the rough wall, waiting for the water to boil, I imagined I could almost feel eyes watching us from the outer darkness. A coyote howled somewhere, and a chill crawled like a centipede up the back of my neck at the mournful sound. Was it a coyote or a band of Apaches creeping up on our fire, waiting for a chance to finish the job of avenging their dead warriors?

Chapter 3

By staying alert, the three of us could fight off an attack from the tunnel as long as our ammunition held out. Ammunition was something we had plenty of — several hundred rounds between me and Wiley. His were .45 caliber for his 7½-inch-barreled Colt and also for my Colt. I also had a supply of .44 center-fire cartridges for my Winchester '73 carbine. It would have been better had all our weapons used interchangeable cartridges, but our foresight in preparing for this trip had not extended to this item. Burke's old Henry rifle took a .44 rim-fire shell. We could possibly be starved out, as our food was short, but we could stretch our water supply for many days by remaining quietly inside, out of the sun.

All these possibilities ran through my mind as I glanced at Wiley. He was supporting Chris's head and helping him sip the hot coffee laced with honey. He had used an extra shirt and strips of blanket to form a crude bandage around the boy's torso and over his shoulder, after pouring alcohol on the wound.

The flickering light of our small fire cast weird, wavering shadows along the roughened walls of the tunnel. The entrance was framed with squared cottonwood logs more than a foot thick. The tunnel itself was about five feet wide and maybe seven feet high. The framing was continued in the drift with upright supports about every ten feet back as far as I could see. I could feel a slight rush of cool, fresh air on my face coming from the depths of the mine.

"This tunnel must connect to the outside somewhere," I remarked to Burke as he handed me a tin cup of steaming coffee.

"Probably a vertical shaft back there," he replied. "That's the way a lot of these mines in the region are dug."

"Looks like somebody put a lot of work into this."

"Somebody maybe found enough ore to look pretty promising. I'd say they either got it all out, or the vein petered out, or maybe the Indians got too dangerous to let 'em keep on working it. Looks to be several years since anybody has worked this one. They probably had to haul the ore quite a distance to have it milled; I don't know of any running water closer by." He gnawed off a piece of jerky and chewed thoughtfully as he stared back into the darkness.

"If we had anything to make a torch out of, we could do some exploring," I said.

"There are small mines being worked over around the San Pedro River west of here," Burke continued. "Don't think anyone has struck it really rich, but I'd suspect there are some good veins of silver being hit. You know how rumors go, though. If I were to believe everything I've heard, I'd be convinced this whole territory was paved with gold and silver and copper."

"Are you looking to do some prospecting yourself?" I inquired when he paused.

"Naw, not really. I've seen too many men get gold-and-silver fever. Drives them crazy. They'd do anything to get it — lie, cheat, steal, even kill. That's no good. Besides, I don't believe I was born to grub in the ground like a prairie dog. No, my ambition lies in another direction. I want to be known for my pictures, for my photographs. This will never last," he shrugged, gesturing at the empty tunnel. "Most men work harder trying to get something for nothing than if they took up some legitimate trade. Even if by some wild chance a man should hit it big, he usually can't keep it. Either he goes crazy and throws it away on extravagant living and winds up dead broke, or somebody schemes him out of it, or he's robbed. Even if he manages to keep it, how can a man in that position know who his friends really are? It's not like you two. You came to my aid when I needed it — for no thought of reward. At least," he added with a slight grin, "if you did expect a reward besides my gratitude, you're going to be sadly disappointed."

"We heard the shots, saw you in trouble, and came to help," I replied simply.

"Oh, don't get me wrong," Burke continued, pulling a short pipe out of the dunnage piled beside his bedroll, "I'd like to be rich, just as anybody else would. But just rich enough so I wouldn't have to struggle for a living the rest of my life. It would be nice to be able to draw a deep breath and not worry about how you're going to make it from one week to the next. Fabulous wealth just brings trouble." He finished packing the pipe bowl from a beaded doeskin pouch, reached for a flaming twig, and applied it to the bowl.

I complimented him on the beautiful work on the tobacco pouch.

"It was given to me by a little girl up in Colorado last year," he replied, blowing a cloud of smoke at the ceiling and leaning back against the thick cottonwood brace. "She liked the photographs I took of her. She and the young man she had eyes for didn't believe the elders' superstition about the camera box being bad medicine. She slipped this pouch to me on the sly in exchange for two or three poses of her I printed for her to keep."

Wiley stepped past us and added a few sticks to the fire from our small pile. The small flicker flared up as the dry wood caught.

"That may not be a good idea," Burke said, indicating the blaze. "The way it lights up this entrance, anybody, Indian or otherwise, out there with a rifle in the dark could fire into the opening and the ricocheting slugs would probably get us all."

I could see Wiley stiffen as he stood over the

seated Burke, and I was poised to intervene, but Wiley finally said, with a trace of irritation, "I need the light to see by. If you want to tend this apprentice of yours in total darkness, you're welcome to try."

"I think I could probably find something to make a torch out of," Burke replied evenly.

"It'd make too much smoke in this passageway," Wiley shot back.

"No, there's a slight draft through here that would suck it out," Burke said.

Wiley started to retort, but I cut in quickly. "What do you need? Maybe I can help."

"Nothing. I'm almost done. Just wanted to be sure that gash wasn't bleeding under the bandage. He's resting, but I wanted to check his color. I've got his feet elevated. He took two cups of hot coffee with honey, and we've got him covered good. I think he's sleeping now. All we can do is wait and watch him."

I leaned over the wounded boy, but could see little in the flickering light of the small fire a few feet behind us.

"Strike a match here so I can check him one more time," Wiley said. I did as requested, raking it across the rocky wall beside me and cupping my hands around the flame, as the draft in the tunnel nearly sucked it out. I held the flame close to the waxen face of the sleeping boy. He didn't appear to be over fifteen. Wiley felt his forehead and his pulse.

"I think he's okay. No thanks to Mr. Burke

here. He seemed more interested in his mules than he did in his apprentice."

Burke turned his head toward us, the fire behind him forming a halo of reddish hair around his silhouetted head.

"I won't justify that with an answer," he said, his voice rising slightly. "You can think what you want. I know next to nothing about medicine, even though I deal with certain chemicals in my work. So I deferred to your expertise. If anyone else had said to me what you just did, I'd whip him 'til he couldn't stand on his feet. Since you and your partner came to our aid when we needed it, I'll let your remark pass."

Wiley stepped toward him, clenching his fists. "Don't do us any favors!" he grated.

"Hold it, boys, that's enough," I said, stepping between them. "We've had enough problems without fighting among ourselves. Besides, I think we're all just tired and on edge."

"You're right," Wiley said, after a few tense moments, letting out his breath in a rush of air. "Sorry. Want another cup of coffee?" he asked the photographer.

"Believe I will. Thanks." He accepted the proffered cup. Wiley poured himself one, emptying the pot, and the three of us sat down on the floor, our backs to the walls, Wiley and I on one side facing Burke on the other.

"You boys never did tell me much about yourselves," Burke said after a few moments of silence. "We've been too busy to talk."

43

"I used to work for *The Chicago Times Herald*." I told him.

"Oh, a reporter."

"Sort of. I worked for that paper as a correspondent covering General Buck's Big Horn and Yellowstone Expedition against the Sioux and Northern Cheyenne in '76. Now I'm a feature writer, rather than a reporter. I'm doing a series of articles for *Harper's Weekly* magazine. Writing as a firsthand observer about the new gold and silver strikes being made in the Arizona Territory, specifically, the southern part of the Territory."

"You must be pretty good at what you do," Burke said.

"Well, I enjoy it, and I get paid for it. A man can't beat a combination like that. Plus, I'm mostly my own boss." I went on to tell him about our participation in saving the visiting Prince Ferdinand Zarahoff of Romania as he traveled up the Mississippi and Missouri rivers by steamboat. An assassination plot had been foiled. The story had been serialized in *Leslie's Illustrated*.

"We were lucky enough to be in the right place at the right time," I concluded.

"So . . . a couple of professional lifesavers."

"Not really. We actually did come upon you by accident. But it turned out to be a fortunate accident."

"It may not turn out to be so fortunate."

"How's that?"

"Not much of a story in me, I'm afraid. But

someday soon somebody will figure out a way to use photographs in newspapers and magazines for illustration."

"Are you working on such an invention?"

"Me? No, I'm not smart enough for that. I'm just a poor, itinerant Irish 'shadow catcher' from New York City who's trying to make enough to live on. My father was killed in a railroading accident five years ago. A brakeman he was, and a good one. But he made one mistake and was crushed to death between two gondolas on the Erie and Lackawanna Road." He paused, staring into the glowing embers of our dying campfire, and sucked at his pipe, which had gone cold.

"I'm afraid I haven't accomplished much to be proud of," he continued slowly. "I did get a job as one of two photographers to accompany the Hayden Geological Expedition two years ago, but that lasted only a few months. Don't get me wrong — I was lucky to get it; had to use a little influence through a local New York politician I knew. And the assignment was great experience. It was just that . . . well . . . I was captivated by this western country and, after a winter back in New York, decided to outfit myself and come west to see if I could make it. Trouble is, there are too many photographers. Every little town between here and the Hudson River used to have its own portrait studio. A lot of them went out of business after the panic of '73, but there are still plenty of them around, competing for the same

45

market. I came along a little too late to catch the biggest part of the boom for the stereoptic views."

I interrupted him. "The landlady in my boarding house in Chicago kept a stereopticon on the marble-top table in her parlor and could sit for hours looking through it at those card-mounted pictures. Never saw anything look so realistic. Don't know how it's done, but it's great. I even bought several sets of pictures for her and the other guests while I was there. There were some fantastic views of the Chicago fire."

"Those pictures have a lot of depth because your eyes and brain are perceiving each duplicate picture at a slightly different angle," Burke replied, warming to a subject he obviously knew well. "I know there's money to be made in stereoscopic views. But the market's been flooded with them. There are thousands of different views and sets of views you can buy on nearly any subject you can think of — from the Pyramids of Egypt to Powell's trip through the Grand Canyon. When those things first came out, they sold for a good price. After the panic of '73, prices dropped a few cents. Now really cheap prints that fade are being sold for a nickel or even two for a nickel." He knocked the dottle out of his pipe against the wooden support behind him and methodically began refilling it from the beaded pouch. "To make it in this business, a man has to become well known, get his name before the public. And the way he does that is by being good enough or lucky enough or have guts enough to get one spectacular picture or series of pictures that will catch the public fancy. Timothy O'Sullivan did it by taking those underground views of the Comstock Mine in 1868, lighting them by means of burning magnesium wire. And William Jackson did it a few years later with his great views of the Yellowstone country, which few people back east had ever seen."

He struck a match to relight his pipe. When he had it going again, he said, "I'm forty years old. If I'm going to make anything of myself, I've got to do it now. I'm looking for that one photo, hopefully a stereoscopic view, that will be unusual enough or spectacular enough to catch the eye of the public and will make my reputation. That's why I'm out here. This country is wild and unsettled. Most of the population is in the east, and those people are hungry for sensational pictures — and stories — of the Wild West."

"I take it you haven't had any luck so far," Wiley said.

"No. I was just breaking even on expenses when this happened." He glanced back into the darkness of the tunnel. "That boy there badgered me for weeks when I was home last winter to take him on as an apprentice. He was bored with school; said he wanted to see the west he had heard so much about. His parents finally consented to his dropping out of school for one year to accompany me and learn what he could of the 'black art,' as some people used to call this trade because a man could blacken his hands working with nitrate of silver." He shook his head regretfully. "The boy's only sixteen. Has two years left in school. Now there's a good chance he'll never get out of this hole alive. Good Lord! What am I going to tell his mother?"

Wiley and I looked at each other. There was nothing to say. Finally, after a few minutes of silence, Wiley stood up and yawned. "I'm dead tired. What say we get these horses back in the mine and hobbled for the night. Don't want to leave any temptation in the way of those Apaches, if any of 'em are still out there. Too bad we don't have anything for the animals to eat," he said, catching the reins of his own mount in the almost total darkness where it was tied just outside the entrance. "But at least we can spare 'em a little water."

I got my own mount, and we watered them from a pan before leading them past the sleeping boy into the blackness of the drift. I was feeling my way along the wall and stopped to strike a lucifer every fifteen or twenty steps to get some idea of where we were going. Somewhere back here that mysterious bearded man had kept a mule. But where? In the sooty blackness of the mine, I was beginning to feel a suffocating panic rising within me. I fought it silently, sucking in the clean, fresh air coming from somewhere ahead. Finally, I felt the wall veer away from my searching hand, and I stopped quickly, afraid of falling into a hole, and struck a match. The brief flare revealed a roughly circular, unsupported space about twenty feet across. Just as the match scorched my fingers and I dropped it, I sensed that the fresh air was coming from above me. I took a few steps forward and looked up. I could just make out a spot of blackness somewhere far above, which was speckled with Arizona stars — a vertical shaft to the outside.

Wiley and I fumbled around in the dark and managed to slip the hobbles on the horses before feeling our way back to the mouth of the tunnel.

I volunteered to take the first watch. Since the Apaches are masters of stealth, I was undecided at first where to station myself. Outside, I would be fair game for a stalking warrior. The same in the wagon. By positioning myself just inside the entrance, I'd never see an attacker until he bounded inside and had a knife in me. We finally decided to move deeper into the tunnel. Wiley and Paddy gently lifted Chris on his blanket without waking the wounded boy and carried him about fifty feet farther back. The two of them bedded down near him.

Then, by lying flat on the hard floor, resting my rifle over a saddle, I could outline the entrance against the starry night sky. Our small fire had died to a few glowing coals. A partial moon had risen and the light outside was slightly more than the stars alone could have accounted for. There was just enough contrast to allow me to silhouette anyone or anything that might try to enter.

As I settled into the prone position, I wondered if I might doze off. It had been a very tiring day.

I needn't have worried. What happened next ensured that I would never go to sleep on watch.

Chapter 4

I had just become aware of the deep, steady breathing of my companions when I was startled by a scratching, scrabbling sound. My heart racing, I rolled around in a vain attempt to penetrate the darkness without striking a match. The sounds faded for a few minutes, but then, with a loud squeaking, something furry brushed past my face and bounded across my shoulder and down my back!

With a stifled yell I jumped up and fumbled for the matches in my vest pocket. As I struck one against the wall, I heard a pistol cocking in the darkness behind me. The match flared, and I held it at arm's length to keep it from blinding me. Two or three small shapes darted through the edges of light.

"Mice!" I breathed, somewhat relieved, although my heart was still pounding. I don't know what I had expected.

"Mice, hell!" Wiley said, coming up softly, gun in hand. "I saw at least one rat."

The match went out, and I struck another. The squeaking and scratching continued in the darkness around us. Reflecting back at us from just beyond the light of the wooden match was a set of baleful red eyes.

51

"*That's* no mouse," Wiley affirmed. At the sound of his voice the eyes blinked out and disappeared.

"Ugly brutes," I shuddered, my skin crawling at the thought of their disease-ridden bites.

"I don't think these desert rats are quite like your big-city rats," Wiley said, letting down the hammer and holstering his Colt. "In fact, the long-tailed kangaroo rat is common to this desert country. They're nocturnal like most desert animals, but they won't bother you."

"Thanks for trying to reassure me," I said, dropping the match as it singed my fingers. "But now that my imagination is stirred up, I can just picture this shaft crawling with all kinds of creatures — centipedes, tarantulas, and the like. I don't think I'll have any trouble staying awake on watch tonight."

"Well, if it's any comfort, there'd be just as many of those things running around and over you if you were sleeping outside there on the ground. It's happened to me before in this territory."

"I guess I was so dead tired on the trail coming out here that they didn't bother me."

"Yeah. Once you got to sleep, there was no waking you."

We stood for a few moments in the darkness without speaking, looking toward the dimly lighted entrance. The squeaking, scratching sounds had receded for the moment. But somewhere outside in the distance the coyotes had started yipping and howling again. It was an eerie, lonesome sound, one that always made me reflective. It was even more so tonight. I was sure my fatigue had something to do with it. As my heartbeat steadied down from the sudden fright, I felt very tired. I wanted very much to walk to the tunnel entrance and stir up the small fire we had let die, but knew that would be a foolish thing to do. Fire would keep the rodents away, but I couldn't afford to waste any more matches. Therefore, I was relieved when Wiley offered to sit up, smoke a pipe, and talk to keep me company for a time. I sat on my saddle and Wiley squatted against the wall as we conversed in low voices in almost total darkness. The glow of our pipes, after we had packed and lighted them, was all but invisible. We talked of several things but the subjects were not as important as the calm, reassuring sound of his voice in the blackness of the mine. He thought the likelihood of a night attack by the raiding band of Apaches was slight. I doubted that he knew any more about it than I did, but it was good to hear anyway. His opinion would not make me relax my vigilance, in any case.

"Do you think that boy Chris has a chance of pulling through?" I asked him when we finally got around to our present situation.

"I wish I knew," he finally replied. "I hope so. I've done all I can, but it may not be enough. Just pray that those Apaches stay off our backs long enough for us to get him to Camp Bowie in the morning. There're regular Army troops there. I hope they have a medical man who can treat him, or it'll be only luck or toughness or his youth that will bring him through. Or maybe all three."

"We need to figure out a way to transport him," I said. "We don't have the use of the wagon, and Burke has no mount, either."

"And we're not even sure where Camp Bowie is from here," Wiley added, without offering a solution to the first problem. "That old man's directions weren't too specific."

"That 'old man' didn't look like he had that many years on him to me — just well used. What do you make of him?"

In the darkness I could sense that Wiley gave his characteristic shrug. "Some sort of prospector, I suppose."

"He looked kind of pale and sick to me," I said.

"I was too busy at the time to really take a good look at him," Wiley said. "Thought he'd probably stay around and we'd get to know him. Didn't know he was gonna skedaddle like that."

"You don't reckon he was on the run from the law, do you?"

"Could be. But I think he'd rather have taken his chances with us here in this mine tunnel for a few hours than chance being sliced up while he was sleeping around some campfire out there."

"Maybe he knows the Indians better than he knows us. For all he knew, we could have been a bunch of murderers."

"Did you notice if he was armed?"

"Don't believe he was — unless he had a saddle gun on that mule or a pocket pistol hidden on him somewhere."

"Can't figure him out. Maybe he's an army deserter from Camp Bowie."

Wiley mulled this over for a minute. "If so, why would he be hanging around this close to the fort? No, he was wearing an old officer's campaign hat all right, but the rest of his clothes weren't military and he didn't get to looking that ratty in a couple of days. He's been out here for a while."

"Well, whoever or whatever he is, he sure saved us. Maybe we'll get a chance to thank him properly someday."

"Yeah." I heard Wiley get up and stretch and yawn. "Time for me to get a little shut-eye. Call me in an hour or two and I'll take the second watch. The photographer can have the last one and stir up a little breakfast for us."

He felt his way back to his bedroll and lay down.

I stared out at the desert landscape that was silvered by a moon now well up. As everything got quiet, the mice and rats got busy again, apparently fighting and squealing and seeing how much noise they could make. A few minutes later, I could feel myself becoming drowsy again, so I moved carefully to the mouth of the tunnel, lay down flat, and slid my head outside for a look. The desert landscape was a silver-gray in the moonlight, beautiful and still. I felt sure that countless life and death struggles were going on out there beyond my sight and hearing, among the nocturnal creatures of this arid land — the owl hunting the mouse, the skunk and bat hunting centipedes and other insects, the bobcat and rattlesnake hunting small rodents. But the only hunter I was concerned with was the human hunter, the craftiest of all. I started at the left limit of my vision and, barely moving anything but my eyes, thoroughly scrutinized a segment of the terrain within my vision, examining every rock and shrub before moving on to the next segment. In this methodical way I covered the entire half-circle of the horizon within my purview. The slopes of the hill nearby and in the middle distance and the dry washes appeared completely deserted, although once or twice I was sure I detected a slight movement in the darkly etched moon shadows. Too small to be a man. Some desert animal, no doubt.

In this way I killed an hour or so, enchanted and almost hypnotized by the beauty of the scene. But my vigilance never relaxed. Even though I was only vaguely aware of the time, I purposely let Wiley sleep through his watch. The moon was well down the sky and a very slight breeze was bringing the fresh smell of sage to my nose before I crept back into the tunnel and roused Burke, handing him his own Henry.

"Everything's quiet," I whispered to him. He

grunted an acknowledgment, took the rifle, and edged away in the darkness. I pulled off my boots and flopped down on my own blankets. I was unconscious before I knew I was even tired.

The next thing I knew, someone was nudging me, and my eyes flew open to full daylight. Wiley was standing over me. "Breakfast." I rolled over, feeling stiff and tired. But the smell of coffee brought me awake quickly as I pulled on my boots. Burke was poking at the small fire. He looked rather owlish from too little sleep. "Coffee laced with honey is about all I can offer this morning, men. Unless you want to soften a little hardtack in it. I'm out of cheese and crackers."

"We've still got a few strips of jerky in our saddlebags," Wiley replied, easing the apprentice back onto his blankets and standing up. "But I'd sure like to sit down to a good breakfast of ham and eggs and grits one of these days. It's been a long time."

"Quit talking like that. My stomach's already growling. Bet I've lost seven or eight pounds on this trip."

But my mind wasn't really on my stomach. I glanced back at the pale Chris and then looked questioningly at Wiley. I had half expected to find the boy dead this morning.

"How is he?" I asked quietly.

"Holding his own," he replied, reaching for the steaming tin cup of black coffee Burke was handing him. "He may even be a little better. He needs medical attention, and that gash needs to be stitched. He's weak from loss of blood, but he's tough." He sipped tentatively at the coffee. "Best thing he's got going in his favor is his youth. You or I wouldn't be doing as well, I'm afraid."

I stepped outside and helped myself to coffee from the smoke-blackened pot steaming on the fire. After I had mixed a dollop of honey into it and dunked a chunk of hardtack, I began to feel better.

"No problems during your watch?" I asked Burke.

"None. Except for those damn mice and the coyotes. I guess those Apaches had had enough."

"Maybe. Maybe not," Wiley remarked, sweeping his eyes over the dry hill outside. The morning sun had cleared the eastern slopes and was already driving off the October-night chill.

"We need to rig something to transport that kid to Fort Bowie," I finally said, as the three of us finished up our skimpy breakfast, and Burke doused our small fire with the dregs of the coffee and some dirt. "Any suggestions?"

No one replied for a minute or two as we all considered our alternatives.

"If we had a couple of long poles we could rig a litter and sling him between the two horses," Wiley said, looking around for some suitable material. "Or we could make a travois." But it was obvious there were no long poles, nor any trees to cut them from.

"What about the wagon?" Burke suggested. "The trace chains are still in place, even though most of the harness is gone. Maybe we could rig up some kind of rope harness that would work."

We considered this for a minute.

"Don't think it would work," I said finally. "Ours aren't draft horses, and that's a heavy wagon, even if we left most of the stuff behind. Besides, I don't think we have enough rope between us to make any kind of harness. We might injure these horses so they couldn't be ridden again."

"Why don't we take one of those planks from the wooden shelves or benches and tie him to that and then lash the whole thing lengthwise onto the back of my horse. He's the bigger of the two," said Wiley.

It sounded feasible, so in short order we had a shelf board of appropriate length and width, pried loose from the ambulance. Wiley, experienced in rigging pack saddles, fashioned a thick pad for the animal's back, and we padded the board as well as we could with blankets, before easing the now-conscious boy onto it and strapping him to it with some tie straps from my McClellan saddle.

Wiley eyed our makeshift stretcher transport critically when it was all in place. "It'll have to do. We shouldn't jar him too much if we walk the horses and stick to the low ground. One of us can walk beside him to make sure it doesn't slip."

"It'd help if we knew exactly where Camp Bowie is from here," Burke said. "One of us could ride ahead and get them to bring an ambulance or wagon back here for Chris."

"That sure sounds like an easier and safer solution," I said, even though we already had the youth in place on Wiley's animal. "Why don't you take a hike up the hill behind the mine here and scout off to the southeast," I suggest to Burke. "See if you can see any sign of it. That old prospector indicated it was only a few miles in that direction."

Without a word he stepped outside. I put on my hat and followed him out into the morning sunshine, leaving Wiley to watch the litter in the shade of the tunnel. I walked a few yards uphill to one side of the mine entrance and covered his climb with my rifle. "Be careful," I cautioned him. "I still have the feeling this pass is crawling with Apaches, fort or no fort."

"Don't worry," he replied, starting his climb among the needle-sharp yucca plants. "The Apache hasn't been weaned who's going to decorate his wickiup with this red mop."

"I don't think the Apaches scalp their victims."

"Whatever they do, they'll pay hell doing it to me!" He grinned wickedly, and I got the distinct feeling he would have welcomed another encounter with the savage raiders who had stolen

60

his mules and almost killed his apprentice. But the warming desert terrain appeared devoid of any human life, as I seated myself on a convenient rock and scanned the scenery. I knew that covering his ascent this way was not only a futile gesture, but probably also very risky. I could have been looking at a half-dozen Indians crouched within my vision on the rocky hillsides, and unless they moved or wanted to be seen, I could not distinguish them from the brown rocks. The thought made me a little jumpy. But my first encounter with Apaches, ending as successfully, if luckily, as it had, probably made me a little careless. I had faith in the inability of any Indian to fire a rifle any distance with accuracy.

The noise above me subsided and the shower of small stones being kicked back down the hill ceased. I looked up. Burke had disappeared over the bulge of the hill. In less than five minutes he came jumping and sliding back down toward me.

"Couldn't see anything," he said as he plunged to a stop near me. "Thought I detected some haze hanging in the air south by east of here among the hills, but couldn't tell if it was smoke or not."

"Let's head for it," I replied as we descended to the drift entrance. "If I know the army, they were up at the crack of dawn. That haze is probably the remains of their early-morning cooking fires." I tried to sound confident.

Wiley had gathered up our bedrolls and

strapped them onto the saddles. We loaded our weapons, filled the gaps in our belt loops with fresh cartridges, filled our canteens, and started our trek back to the stage road to get our bearings. Wiley led the horse bearing the injured boy, and I led my saddled gelding with Wiley's saddle and gear tied awkwardly atop it. Burke plodded along between us, carrying nothing but his old Henry and a two-quart canteen full of water. Wiley and I had watered the horses before starting.

We retraced our steps of the day before for about a mile east where we struck the stage road again and turned right. The coach road followed a winding course to the southwest through the bottom of a sandy, brushy canyon. It was more of a meandering wash than a stage road, with the hillsides sloping back on either side. The trail proved to be a gradual but steady climb and our feet dragged in the soft sand. The sun cleared the tops of the hills to our left and bore down in the windless air, bringing out the sweat on our backs and under our hatbands. We had to pause frequently to uncap our canteens for the wounded apprentice, who was moaning for water. I was glad we hadn't tried to drag the photographer's wagon along with us.

After an hour or so, we stopped to rest and assess the situation.

"There's got to be some kind of a road or trail into this fort," I said, adjusting the hat on Chris to keep the sun out of his eyes. Wiley was busy checking the lashings on the makeshift litter. The boy seemed to be half-dozing.

"Do you think we're going in the right direction?"

"Don't know of any way we could climb out of this canyon," Burke said. "We couldn't have passed it."

"We can't be too far from it, judging from what the miner said," Wiley concluded, removing his hat and wiping a sleeve across his forehead.

We all took another drink of water and without another word, trudged on. As I glanced back over my shoulder, I noticed we were closed in by the screen of brush and trees alongside the winding wash. I would have given almost anything at that moment if a celerity mail coach had come along, if for no other reason than to reestablish contact with the outside world. What a beautiful place this canyon bottom would be for an Apache ambush, I thought, as I casually swept my eyes over the crests of the hills a couple of hundred yards away on either side of us. I didn't voice my uneasiness to the others. The only sound in the silence was our heavy breathing and our boots and the horses' hooves crunching in the gravel or now and then striking a small stone. I saw my companions also glancing around and up at the hillsides.

Just then the mouth of a side canyon opened up on our left. The declivity angled steeply upward and was very rocky and cactus-covered.

There was no trail up this canyon, but after a hurried discussion, we decided to take this side canyon since it tended in the general direction the stranger had indicated. At least it led upward where we could get a better view of the surrounding country.

It turned out to be at least a mile of the most grueling climb through broken rocks and spiny plants. We were sweating and panting heavily, taking turns leading the horses and steadying the load that was the wounded boy. I was finally on the point of saying something reassuring, just to break the oppressive silence, when I looked up and saw the adobe walls of a large corral to the right. A few more yards and we emerged from the steep canyon and there, before us, cupped in an opening in the surrounding hills, lay Fort Bowie.

Chapter 5

It was as welcome a sight as I had seen for many a day. The quadrangle of buildings that made up the post lay roughly one hundred yards to the right of where we emerged from the canyon.

I turned and grinned at Wiley and Burke. "Nothing to it if you only follow your nose."

"I've had to do just that a few times since I've been in this territory," Burke commented.

We started forward up the slope, still leading the horses. Before we had gone much more than fifty yards, we were challenged by a sentry. We stopped in our tracks, showing our hands and our good intentions.

"We're friendly!" Burke shouted. "We've got an injured boy here."

The blue-clad soldier eased the hammer down on his Springfield and came trotting toward us. He glanced over us quickly and his eyes fastened on the apprentice strapped precariously to the back of Wiley's horse.

"Follow me," the trooper said, turning and starting back toward the post. I was thankful he didn't ask a lot of questions.

A few minutes later we were talking to an officer, a tall, sunburned lieutenant with a drooping mustache, explaining briefly what had happened. He, too, asked no questions.

"Fetch Dr. Donnelly," he commanded an orderly. The orderly threw a quick salute and ran toward an L-shaped adobe building that formed the northwest corner of the quadrangle. The building had been whitewashed to reflect the sometimes fierce Arizona sun. Meanwhile, Burke, Wiley, and the officer, a Lieutenant Warren, were unstrapping the board Chris was on and easing it off the horse. Evidently the wound had partially reopened in spite of our care, since blood was beginning to soak through the makeshift bandage. The boy's eyes opened and closed, but didn't focus on us, and he seemed oblivious to what was happening to him.

Just then the post surgeon came striding up. He wore no hat or coat, only a white shirt and his blue uniform trousers stuffed into polished boots. He was short and broad-chested and had an honest, open, intelligent face. The black hair and thick mustache had just a touch more gray than I remembered, but it was without a doubt the same Dr. Kenneth Donnelly from General Buck's campaign against the Sioux in '76. I was confused. How had this man, who was with the Third Cavalry last year, suddenly appeared here at a remote outpost in the Arizona Territory with the Sixth Cavalry? He hardly looked at me, and I'm sure he wouldn't have recalled me anyway, since our only meeting, when he treated me for a slight hand wound, had been brief. Under the circumstances, I didn't feel this was the time to renew an acquaintance or ask any questions about his presence.

"He got slashed across the chest by an Apache knife," Burke said. He hesitated. "Do you think it's terminal?"

The doctor glanced at the redhead and snorted. "Living is terminal," he said shortly. "Wounds may be fatal."

"The doc will take good care of him," Lieutenant Warren said as we started to follow the orderlies who were bearing Chris on his board into the post hospital. "I'll escort you to Major Curwen McCullough." His offer was polite enough, but more in the nature of a command.

Burke looked uncertainly at the retreating backs of Dr. Donnelly and the orderlies carrying his apprentice, then fell in behind us as the lieutenant led us west across the packed bare earth of the parade ground to a low adobe building that turned out to be the adjutant's office. Lieutenant Warren opened the wooden plank door and entered first. He saluted, then stepped aside as we entered the low-ceilinged room. In spite of the mild October morning outside and the open windows, the air was uncomfortably warm.

"Sir, these men have brought in a wounded boy. Said they were attacked by Apaches nearby."

I half expected the adjutant to be no more than a captain but the man behind the desk must have been the post commander since he wore the bars of a major on his blue tunic.

Placing the pen he was holding across the pronged holder attached to a bottle of Carter's ink, he leaned forward on a small stack of papers, his heavy eyebrows knitted in a frown. The iron gray hair and the huge salt-and-pepper mustache that hid his mouth belied the youthful appearance of his smooth, unlined face.

"Let's hear it," he commanded briefly, fixing a stare on Burke, who was standing in front.

The photographer summarized the events of the past day while the commander hardly shifted his gaze, except to glance at me and Wiley when our part in the narrative arrived.

"Damn!" The expletive exploded from somewhere under the massive mustache. He was silent as he stared at the far wall, drumming the fingers of his left hand on the desk. I could feel sweat beginning to trickle down my back in the close atmosphere.

"How badly is the boy hurt?" he finally asked without looking around.

"I don't know," Burke replied.

"The surgeon is looking after him, sir," Lieutenant Warren added.

"Anyone else hurt?" the major inquired, dragging his eyes back to us.

"No."

"Lieutenant, send a patrol with a team of mules to bring the wagon in here. Take one of these men to help locate it. Put these men up in the officers' quarters." Then to us, "I'll talk with you again after you've rested and eaten."

He stood up, signaling an end to the interview. Lieutenant Warren saluted and led us out the door into the welcome fresh air.

"Sergeant Johnson, notify me immediately when that early patrol returns," I heard Major McCullough say as we retreated across the parade grounds toward the officers' quarters.

It seemed strange and somewhat uncomfortable to find myself again within the confines of a military post. Even though I had been a civilian war correspondent at the time, I was still guilty of having aided the escape and desertion of an officer who had been arrested pending court martial. This had happened near the end of General Buck's campaign in the Dakota Territory over a year ago. I felt that I had done the right thing at the time and would not have given it a second thought now, except for the fact that Dr. Kenneth Donnelly, who was on that campaign and was doubtless aware that Wiley and I were involved, was now serving at this post manned by the Sixth Cavalry in a remote part of the Arizona Territory. Damn the luck, anyway!

I glanced at Wiley who was eyeing the blue-clad troopers moving within the quadrangle. His face indicated his uneasiness as well. We had originally planned to stop at this post to get the latest news of Indian problems and prospecting activities in the area, while we restocked our water from the spring and our provisions from the sutler's store. But now we were practically being ordered into confinement until we could be questioned further by the post commander. Things were not going as planned, and I began to get a trapped feeling, almost as strong as the claustrophobia that came over me when we were penetrating the blackness of the mine tunnel last night.

An orderly took our two horses to the stable and we were shown to the long, low adobe building with the wooden porch that comprised the officers' barracks on the upper side of the sloping parade ground. We dumped our bedrolls and saddlebags on the bunks and Burke followed the lieutenant back out to guide the detail to his wagon.

"Mess call at twelve, gentlemen," Lieutenant Warren said over his shoulder. "Mess is that way. Just follow the crowd."

I propped open the door to get some fresh air after they left, and Wiley threw himself down on the gray army blanket covering one of the bunks. "Wish we could just get our provisions and water and be on our way," Wiley said half-aloud.

"I have the same feeling."

"Dare we go to the mess hall? There may be some others here besides Dr. Donnelly from General Buck's command who would recognize us. We could still be held by the civil authorities for aiding the escape of a military prisoner — the man who is now my brother-in-law," he added.

"To hell with it. Where's your sense of adventure? I'm hungry. I'm so sick of hardtack and jerky, I could boil one of my boots and eat it, with some mesquite, just for variety. I don't know what Dr. Donnelly's doing here, but this is the Sixth Cavalry, not the Third. Maybe they were short of doctors and transferred him, but the chances of anyone else from General Buck's campaign up north being here are mighty slim." I wasn't totally convinced myself, but Wiley seemed to relax and we discussed our situation further, including the possible identity and whereabouts of the mysterious, bearded miner who had saved our lives at the time. I had stretched out on the bunk across from Wiley's. Our desultory conversation lessened as weariness overtook us. The stress I had been under, combined with my lack of sleep the night before and this morning's two-hour march, finally caught up with me, and I slept.

The next thing I heard was the bugler blowing mess call. I didn't want to move; I felt as if I had just closed my eyes. But I rolled over and put my booted feet on the floor, as Wiley was reluctantly doing the same. We rubbed our eyes and stretched, put our hats on, and headed outside in the direction of some real food.

The post was not large, probably fewer than three hundred men, I guessed. And some of them must have been out on patrol and various other detached duties, since the mess hall was far from full. I still felt curious eyes on us as we went through the line of the mess hall next to the cavalry barracks. We found a table as close as possible to empty, but a young private sitting across from us took it as his duty to be friendly.

"You aren't new recruits, are you?" he asked. He had a fresh-faced look and frankness about him that spoke of a midwestern farm.

"Just passing through," I mumbled around a mouthful of stew.

"Didn't think they'd send recruits here with no uniforms. Thought maybe you were civilian scouts."

I could feel other heads turning to look in our direction. One sergeant, in particular, had a vaguely familiar look about him, but I kept my head down, concentrating on my food, and answered the private only in monosyllables and grunts until he lost interest and quit talking. We ate our fill as quickly as possible without appearing to rush and then retired to our quarters again.

About an hour later, the detail returned, Burke driving two Army mules that were pulling his converted ambulance.

"Nothing else was bothered," he said, as he and a private unhitched the span of mules in front of our wooden porch.

"Except for the spilled chemicals, some dried blood, and a few bullet holes, she's as good as new." He looked fondly at his rolling home, which still had an arrow protruding from a back door.

As one soldier led the team of mules away, with two more carrying the harness toward the stables, a corporal approached us from the other direction. He gave us a halfhearted salute, waving a hand in the direction of the brim of his kepi. "Major would like to see you in his quarters."

"Right now?" Burke asked. "I was just going over to the hospital to check on my apprentice."

The corporal shrugged, as if the whole thing were of vast indifference to him. "Just carrying out my orders. I was told to fetch you."

"Well, I guess a few more minutes won't make any difference," Burke conceded. "Let's go." As we followed the corporal, I realized that we were going in the opposite direction of the office where we had first met Major McCullough. About a hundred yards from our quarters, just back from the upper corner of the quadrangle on a rise overlooking the post, stood an imposing two-story frame house that apparently was the home of the commanding officer and his family. We went up several steps to the porch and then were shown into a very commodious parlor, furnished with stuffed horsehair furniture and a couple of rocking chairs. A fireplace was set into one wall, and near the front windows, which were hung with white lace curtains, stood a marble-topped table containing an oil lamp, a Bible, and a stereopticon. When Burke's eyes alighted on the picture viewer, he immediately went over and picked it up. A box of card-mounted double-image photographs was with it, and he slipped one into the holder and holding it to his eyes, turned his back to the window to view it in the light.

"Some fine views of the city of Paris, are they not?" remarked the major as he entered the parlor from another room. "Very realistic. A very good way for my wife and I to travel. Relieves many weary hours at this godforsaken post." He waved a hand at us. "Sit down, sit down. Make yourselves comfortable."

He seemed much more relaxed and congenial in his own home in shirt-sleeves than he had this morning. Maybe he had to appear tough and formal in front of his men. He offered us cigars, and we accepted. The corporal had disappeared.

"I took the liberty of checking on your young friend," the major said when we were all comfortably seated, our cigars glowing. "Dr. Donnelly tells me he's going to be fine. He's weak from loss of blood, but the doctor has just finished stitching that nasty gash and says he just needs rest and nourishment. He may have some numbness along that scar later, where some nerves were cut, but nothing serious. He told me the boy should make a full recovery." He smiled. "What are your plans now?" he asked, looking from one of us to the other.

"My immediate problem, Major, is to find a team of mules or horses to pull my wagon to Tucson," Burke replied. "And my second problem is even bigger — finding the money to pay for it."

The major stroked his chin thoughtfully for a moment. "Well, I think we've got some extra stock we can let you have, but the army won't let me turn 'em loose on credit. You say you're a photographer? Maybe we can work out some arrangement. I've been wanting to make a permanent pictorial record of Fort Bowie. And I'm sure some of the officers and men might want a portrait for the folks back home. Do you still have all your gear?"

"Yes, sir. I've got all my cameras intact. And I believe I still have enough hypo left to do the job. In fact," Burke grinned, "I can take some stereoscopic views of the fort, which you can add to your collection here."

"Good. Just keep track of your normal charges and we'll work out an arrangement and take care of the paperwork." The major's tone was businesslike.

On impulse I said, "We can let you have some money until you get back on your feet." I didn't know what Wiley's reaction would be, but Burke didn't strike me as a deadbeat.

Burke nodded. "Thanks."

"We're continuing on over toward the San Pedro district," I said, glancing at Wiley and getting a barely perceptible nod, as though we had not specifically discussed our immediate plans. "And, under the circumstances, I think it would be wise to travel with Paddy Burke."

"Feel free, of course, to use whatever facilities we have, while you're here," the major continued. "The maximum complement of this post is only three companies — two of cavalry and one of infantry. Besides being understrength,

75

about a third of our men are out on patrol right now, so you won't find yourselves crowded. Looking after the civilian travelers and protecting this road and the spring are the reasons this post was put here fifteen years ago. Boring and hot as it is much of the time, we still have an important job here."

It struck me that he was trying to convince himself as much as he was us.

The commandant puffed on his cigar and blew a cloud of smoke at the ceiling. "That's why I was so surprised and irritated this morning when I heard about your run-in with that band of renegades. Things have been relatively quiet during this past summer and fall. Geronimo and his followers are in the mountains in Mexico, and we've had only a few raids on scattered ranches across the line into the territory. The reservation Indians — God knows why — haven't kicked up much of a fuss at San Carlos."

At this point a lady entered the room, bearing a tray and glasses. She moved gracefully as she set the tray on a round wooden table in the center of the room. She appeared to be about forty, slim and fairly attractive, with her graying, thick chestnut hair swept back and fastened behind her head. She wore a long-sleeved, light dress that brushed the floor. Her entrance was so quiet it was almost like an apparition.

The three of us rose automatically.

"Gentlemen, may I present my wife, Rosa," the major said. "I thought you might like some-

76

thing cool to drink. It's only lemon-sugar with our fresh spring water added, and we have no ice, but I thought it might provide a welcome change." He went on to introduce us individually, and each of us mumbled our greetings. I suddenly felt self-conscious at my unshaven and unwashed appearance. She acknowledged us and, smiling, glided out of the room again.

The lemon-sugar drink was very tart and good. The cigar, I noticed, was as good as any smoke I had ever tasted — every bit as good as the cigars available on the elegant riverboat we had ridden up from New Orleans last summer.

"A very attractive lady, your wife," Burke commented.

"Thank you. And very long-suffering, I might add. I've promised her a trip back east to visit her people this coming year. I hope the Apaches don't hinder those plans. Which brings me back to the immediate problem. A routine patrol of thirty men, one noncom and one officer, left at dawn this morning to make a swing out to the west of here, scouting for just such renegade bands as you encountered."

He went on to question us closely as to the appearance and number of the attacking Indians. Each of us contributed bits and pieces of what we remembered of the dress and weapons of the marauding band.

"Hard to say just what band they came from. Renegade Apaches from the San Carlos Reservation, probably. They're either holed up in the

Chiricahuas just southwest of here or were headed back for Mexico when they left you. They might have been on their way back from another raid on one of the ranches north of here, when you had the bad luck to run into them, and they decided to take home a prize of a team of good mules. What they're mainly after is horses, mules, guns, and ammunition. I'm sorry some of our troops couldn't have been there to stop the attack on you, but with only three understrength companies of men to cover many square miles of this rough country, you see . . ." He shrugged and sipped from his glass. "If you want my advice," he continued, "you'll head straight for Tucson when you leave here. Even with the Indians relatively quiet in the south at the moment, no one can predict how long that will last. As you just found out, no one can guarantee safety. Your lives may be in jeopardy every hour, day and night."

"What about all these prospectors I've been hearing about for the past few months?" I asked. "Who's protecting them?"

"More than a few of them have been found tortured and killed by Apaches and eaten by the coyotes. One or two of them had been working out of the newly established Fort Huachuca, about sixty miles southwest of here. The Apaches eventually got them nonetheless. We do the best we can, but our primary responsibility is to protect the stages and the mail through the pass."

He had begun to sound like he was quoting from his orders. He was trying to tell us we were on our own. But we had never doubted this, and never asked for army protection.

"I'd like to be able to provide you with an escort to Tucson, but I don't think I can spare the men," he continued as if reading my thoughts. "Maybe I can get you an escort with the next mail stage going west if . . ."

"Never mind, Major," I interrupted. "We'll make our own way. If there's so much danger, who was it that dug and worked that mine where we hid out last night?"

"That's just what I'm talking about. That gold mine was discovered and worked successfully maybe twenty years ago by a Colonel Stone and some other men. They were doing well, had set up a mill to crush the ore and were hauling it to Tucson, but the Apaches soon put an end to that. Murdered every man of them. What's left is what you saw. Don't doubt but what there's still a good bit of gold in there, and it'll be found in a few years when it's safe enough to thoroughly work this area again."

"What about this character who saved our skins?" Wiley Jenkins asked. "You know anything about him?"

"Some of my officers have reported seeing a man such as you describe. He usually runs and tries to hide from our patrols. Some sort of crazy prospector, I would suspect."

"How long has he been around here?" I asked.

"Let's see . . . I guess I first heard about him over a year ago. My own theory as to why he's survived traveling alone in hostile country is that the Indians know he has nothing to steal except an old mule and a dog that sometimes travels with him. He's no threat to the hostiles and they know it. The Apaches might even admire his courage.

"The Apache warriors who jumped you are diehards who won't accept the inevitability of white settlement in this region. That's why these holdouts such as Geronimo and his followers are holed up in the mountains and refuse to come into the reservations. That's why they are taking vengeance on any whites they can find — especially ranchers and miners who are taking the land for permanent settlement. Then again, the Apaches need horses and anything else they can steal, in addition to punishing the white interlopers and proving their manhood. These raids also help scare off any other would-be settlers."

"Are there any new settlements springing up between here and Tucson, Major?"

"Small groups of prospectors are banding together for protection. We get some spotty information now and then over our new telegraph — when it's working — about new strikes and stampedes, so we can keep up with the movements of the civilian population. On my last trip to Tucson, a month ago, I discovered that quite a few small claims had been filed recently in the southern part of the territory. I don't think they've founded any new towns lately — just some rough mining camps. But who knows what they'll become, in time, if the mines prove out."

"We may do a little prospecting, ourselves," Wiley said. "That was the main reason we came to the territory."

"Well, there's a small group of miners just a few miles west of here on the other side of the pass," the major said. "But they may not be welcoming any newcomers. My patrols tell me they're standing armed guards."

"Probably just protecting themselves from the Apaches," Burke said.

"That, and one more menace that's been plaguing the various camps and small towns the past few weeks," Major McCullough said.

"What menace?"

"There's an outlaw plaguing the small towns and mining camps. Word is that he and four or five of his men have been rustling for a living and then retreat across the border for a refuge from the law. Mostly they just walk into a town or camp and bully the population into giving them anything they want. And they always have the firepower and the gall to make it stick."

"Mexican bandits?" Burke inquired.

"There are a couple of Mexicans in the gang, but the main one is a white man. A really mean one." Curwen McCullough grinned. "Now I guess I've given you enough to worry about. If you took everything I've said seriously, you'd head back east at the earliest opportunity.

'Course, if I were a few years younger and foot-loose, I'd be out looking for pay dirt the same as you, and the devil take the hindmost."

I drained my glass and looked around the room. With its civilized furnishings, rugs, framed pictures on the walls, and other amenities, I might have been sitting in some comfortable home in Ohio or Kentucky or Pennsylvania. Glancing outside the curtained front windows was the only thing that brought me back to the harsh reality of this desert land that was being wrested, inch by inch and year by year, from the Apaches.

"Gentlemen," the major was saying, "I appreciate your sharing my hospitality this afternoon, and if there is anything I can do to make your stay here more pleasant, just give the word."

Chapter 6

"Here, hold this." Burke handed me a wet glass photographic plate, completely enclosed in a light-tight frame. His big, square, wooden camera with its black bellows was perched atop a tripod on a windy ridge overlooking Fort Bowie from the west. Burke flipped back the black cover draped over the camera, took the frame from me and, with a deft motion, slid it into a slot and withdrew the frame cover, leaving the glass plate inside the camera. He ducked his head under the black drape, out of the bright sun, and checked the focus. Then he reached around and uncapped the lens, timing the action with his pocket watch in the other hand. After an exposure of about five seconds, he recapped the brass tube protruding from the front of the camera. He took the frame cover from me and retrieved the glass plate, still sealed from the light.

"Have to work fast," he said, scrambling down the rocky trail from the ridge, toward his wagon parked a few hundred feet below. I lifted the big camera off the tripod, set it on the ground, and hurried after him.

"In this desert air, the plates dry almost faster than I can develop them," he was saying over his shoulder. The wind was nearly whisking his words away. "It's worse in the summer heat. If that happens, the picture's ruined."

He reached the wagon, jumped in, and shut the back doors behind him.

A few minutes later he emerged, wiping his hands on a towel. "Got it. It's a good shot. I'll print it later. Want to make a few more exposures while the sun is high."

It was five days later and we were still marking time at Fort Bowie while Burke attempted to earn the team of two mules Major McCullough had agreed to provide.

"Now you know why I need a helper," the photographer remarked as he brought out his smaller stereoscopic camera. "Let's get up there and bring down that big camera and tripod. We'll get a view from closer in — maybe from the corner of the sutler's store or near the corral. I'll get several of those troopers who just rode in from patrol to hold their horses still for a couple of seconds. Get the parade ground and some of the buildings in the background. The major'll love these three-dimensional views of his command. Something to keep when he retires — show to his counterparts."

We brought the big camera and tripod down from the ridge, and put the heavy camera away. I trudged on down toward the adobe-and-rock sutler's store, the largest building on post, while Burke ducked into his wagon to prepare two more plates for exposure. He had been showing me earlier and attempting to explain something of the science of photography, which was only a few years out of its infancy. Not being familiar with chemicals, I didn't understand a lot of what he told me, but basically, light darkens silver nitrate. In order to have something portable on which to form an image, a glass plate was used. In order to make silver nitrate adhere evenly to the plate when it was held upright, a sticky substance called collodian, containing potassium bromide and potassium iodide, was spread evenly over the glass and allowed to dry. Prior to using the plate in the camera, it was immersed in a solution of silver nitrate, put in a light-tight frame, inserted while wet into the camera and exposed, then taken, still wet, into a darkroom and developed in a solution of water and gallic acid. The developing process was stopped with hyposulphite of soda, the plate rinsed in water and allowed to dry. During the whole process, the wet plate had to be handled with the utmost care to keep bugs and dust and light from it. I didn't really understand what chemical action took place, or even the names of some of the chemicals; I just memorized the process. And I had seen the results. Paddy Burke had not only the brain of a chemist; he had the eyes and soul of an artist. The beautifully proportioned and detailed prints were a joy to behold.

I was beginning to get a little restless. It was time to be moving on. Chris had developed a festering infection in his wound and Dr. Donnelly had been forced to open, drain, and try to sterilize it. The apprentice, it appeared, would not be in any shape to travel for at least two weeks.

"Think I'll make some exposures of the major and his wife this afternoon and then knock off tomorrow and get all of these printed. I've got plenty of paper. I can show you that phase of the operation."

"How long before you get your mules?"

"Depends on what Major McCullough thinks of all these prints when I get them ready to show him. My normal prices, counting a few I've done for individual soldiers, should come close to what I paid for a span of mules at Prescott a few months ago." He slid the wet plate into the small, twin-barreled stereoscopic camera. "I'd like to have a team of four mules; they pull a lot better in sandy soil. And this wagon is heavy — more than a ton fully loaded." He swiveled the camera on its tripod.

"Hey, soldier, hold it right there and I'll get a photograph of you!"

Three days later, the westering sun was casting our long shadows behind us on the copper-colored desert terrain. I pulled my dun to a halt and squinted under my hat brim at the cluster of tents and brush lean-tos clustered against the base of a hill a few hundred yards ahead.

Wiley and I were scouting about a half-mile ahead of Burke's converted ambulance/photographic studio. Wiley rode over to me and we both looked through the partial screen of mesquite that bordered a dry creek bed immediately in front of us.

When it became apparent that Chris would not recover sufficiently to travel, Paddy Burke had decided to leave him in the capable hands of Dr. Kenneth Donnelly and return for him later. After we had spoken with Dr. Donnelly a few more times, he had recognized us from General Buck's campaign. However, he was not interested in reporting us to any military authority. "What civilians do is their own business," was his comment. In fact, I think he was more of a civilian at heart, since he had resigned his commission the year before, but had been persuaded to come back into the service a few months ago and had been assigned to the Sixth Cavalry at Fort Bowie, where his skills could presumably be put to good use.

We had left the fort early this morning and traveled with a routine patrol for about three miles before the soldiers veered southwest toward the Dragoon Mountains. We had continued west until late afternoon found us staring at this camp.

"This must be the camp Major McCullough told us we'd run into," Wiley said, pulling his mount up next to mine.

"Right. 'Cause there's one of those two knobs on the mountain behind it that he said goes by the name of Dos Cabezas."

"Doesn't look like two heads to me."

"You can't see the other one from this angle, but I guess the Spaniards must've had better imaginations."

Distant figures of men were visible, swarming over the sides of the hill, some tunneling horizontally, some attacking the foothills from the top. I could see one of them manning a crude windlass, hauling buckets of ore up from a shaft. Down in the valley, someone in the back of a wagon was knocking apart the boards of a packing crate, apparently to use as firewood or building material. To one side was a flat frame containing drying adobe bricks.

"Has all the frenzy of an anthill," Wiley observed.

"Yeah. Somebody must've struck some good ore here."

"About as unlikely-looking a piece of desert as I've ever seen," Wiley grunted.

"The Comstock wasn't exactly a choice-looking piece of real estate before somebody discovered that hill was filled with silver."

"You're right."

Just then, the photographer's wagon came rolling up.

"So that's Dos Cabezas," Burke said, allowing the tired mules to come to a stop. "Plenty of room to camp. Hope there's some water. That streambed looks dry."

"I doubt if they'd be in the process of building any kind of permanent dwellings if there weren't some source of water."

"Well, let's get on over there and find out," the always impatient Burke said.

Wiley and I rode along the creek bank until, about a mile farther along, we found an easy crossing point for the wagon. It was evidently the commonly used crossing, since the dry, sloping banks had been further broken down by the hooves and wheels of many horses and wagons.

As we halted on a flat spot near the edge of the encampment, two men with Winchesters across their arms came walking up, eyeing us and the gaudy sign on the side of Burke's wagon.

"You gents just passin' through?" one of them inquired.

"Who wants to know?" Burke shot back.

"*We* do," answered the shorter of the two men, who was dressed like a miner.

"Haven't really decided yet," I cut in lightly, swinging stiffly down from my horse. I didn't want to start any trouble here, at least until we had made the acquaintance of these prospectors and had gotten the lay of the land. I hadn't discussed it with Burke, but I hoped to persuade him to linger here a few days while Wiley and I did a little prospecting. I hoped to convince the redhead that he could make some sellable photographs of a raw mining camp in its early stages. My articles would also have the ring of authenticity if I got some personal experience at desert prospecting.

"We're not looking t'welcome any newcomers," the other man added.

89

"Looks like you got a few here already," Wiley said, also dismounting. "We were just on our way to Tucson from Fort Bowie," Wiley continued. "Major McCullough told us you were here and that it might be wise to camp here for protection. We had a run-in a few days ago with a band of renegades in Apache Pass."

"Well . . . I guess that's all right, then," the first man conceded rather grudgingly. "You'll find a pool or two o' water on down that streambed a ways. It's pretty gamey, but it'll do for your animals. And for you, too, if you're thirsty enough."

"Speaking of something wet, where does a man get a drink around here?" Wiley asked.

I shot him a hard look, hoping to deter him, but he wasn't looking.

"That biggest tent up there is the saloon," the short man replied, jerking his head in the general direction of the camp.

The taller of the two men, who was wearing rough, dirty clothes, but was clean shaven, had his hair parted in the middle, and wore a neatly trimmed black mustache, had been eyeing Burke's wagon. "Mister, how does a man go about gettin' his picture took?"

"Just say the word, pry a five-dollar gold piece out of yer pocket and wait 'til the sun comes up in the morning," the Irishman promptly replied as if he had rehearsed the answer.

The tall man, who had a toothpick in the corner of his mouth, grinned, revealing tobacco-stained teeth. "Think I'll just do that very thing. We'll look you up tomorrow before you move on. My name's Charley Singleton. This here's my partner, Bob Welch."

The two men, their curiosity apparently satisfied, turned and walked off toward the camp.

The sun had slid even lower by the time we got Burke's team unhitched and our horses unsaddled. We rubbed them down with some old rags out of Burke's wagon, and then led them west and south along the creek bed for a few hundred yards, where we found the scummy green pools of stagnant water the man had described. As we stood there feeling the late October warmth begin to fade with the coming of night, the sky seemed to get brighter. I looked up at one of the most beautiful sunsets I had ever seen. Flaming red and gold and rose reflections stretched from the western horizon to the meridian in gradually changing shapes and shades. It was a sight that made us all stand in speechless awe. The pink-tinged clouds, with shafts of golden sunlight lancing through them, gradually gave way to a sheen of rose and gold fading into the blue of the heavens.

A shout and raucous laughter came faintly to my ears from the camp as the beehive of humanity behind us went about its usual business, apparently oblivious to the common but gorgeous dying of the desert day.

The horses and mules had drunk their fill and were now browsing on the pale green mesquite leaves and what little grass they could find.

As the sunset faded and darkness began to settle in, we gathered up our animals and brought them back to our camp where we picketed them near the wagon after giving each of them a few handfuls of grain. We gathered some dry brush and kindled a small cooking fire, frying up potatoes, corn, and bacon. As we ate, we watched some of the miners dragging themselves back from their diggings, most of them having worked until it was too dark to see anything. A few even continued on by the light of lanterns, burning the precious coal oil that no doubt had to be hauled in from as far away as Tucson.

"Those must be the newcomers who haven't struck anything yet," Wiley commented, as he poured himself another cup of coffee.

"Maybe so. But do you remember the long hours we worked on that small claim we had in the Black Hills?"

"Yeah," he grinned. "I've never worked so hard in all my life for so little gain. It was fun, though. Thought I was getting something for nothing because I was sluicing it out of that creek gravel instead of getting paid cash to do all that shoveling."

"I guess it was a little different with us," I said. "We were trying to beat winter to what was left in that claim." But deep inside, I had to admit that the fever of the yellow metal had laid hold of me just as hard for a time as it was now apparently gripping those men grubbing on the hillside by the firefly specks of lantern light.

"Think I'll wander up and see what this camp looks like," Wiley said a few minutes later, as he finished his coffee, scooped some clean sand into his tin cup, and scoured it out with his shirttail.

"I'll go, too," I said, getting up.

"You don't think I'm going to bed this early," Burke remarked. "I need to get up there and stir up a little business. If you don't mine the mines, then mine the miners."

"You make yourself sound like one of those vultures who follows the mining camps and railroad boomtowns," I remarked. "You've got a legitimate product to sell."

He grinned. "That's right. Photographers have been welcomed since the gold rush of '49. Who is it who doesn't feel a need to be immortalized on film for posterity?"

Wiley and I were armed with our Colts, but Paddy Burke chose to leave his heavy gunbelt in the wagon and carry only a derringer he wore in a pocket sewn inside his vest. We were all somewhat cleaner than the men who made up this camp, since we had had the advantage of a bath yesterday in the plentiful waters from the spring that filled the water tanks at the fort. We had also washed our clothes and shaved. Because of this, I felt almost like a dandy as we stepped into the big saloon tent a few minutes later and were surrounded by the grubby, unshaven men who were washing the dust out of their throats and re-laxing there.

All conversation stopped and all eyes were riveted on us as we came into the lantern light of the open-sided shelter. It was a few seconds before my eyes could adjust and make out the fifteen or twenty men who stood at the plank bar that was suspended across two barrels, or who perched on boxes, or sat cross-legged on the ground. All of them appeared to be armed. Three lanterns were suspended from the ridge-pole of the tent. A single bartender stood behind the plank and served drinks in tin cups and shot-glasses. His entire stock appeared to consist of two cases of bottles on the ground behind him. Large black letters emblazoned across the wooden cases identified the product as JACK DANIELS TENNESSEE WHISKEY.

"Looks like he serves a good product," Wiley remarked to me under his breath as he spotted the whiskey at the same time I did. "Although I can't say much for the saloon."

"I don't think they're worried about the surroundings," I replied quietly. The faces turned in our direction were curious and not particularly friendly. I knew what they were thinking — more people meant more competition for the available mineral and the necessity for guarding whatever claims had already been staked. I looked around for the two men who had accosted us when we first rode in. They were there, but showed no sign of recognition or welcome.

Finally, after a few awkward seconds, Wiley stepped up to the bar. "I'll have a whiskey."

The small, wizened barman looked up at him. "Ya got sumpin' to pour it in? I'm outa glasses."

"How much for a bottle?"

"Ten dollars."

Wiley hesitated, and I saw his Adam's apple move up and down as he swallowed hard. But he dug into a side pocket and pulled out four quarter eagles. The bartender promptly raked the gold coins off the plank and dropped them into his pocket, then reached into a case and set a sealed, square bottle in front of Wiley.

"Got any water?" Wiley asked.

The skinny bartender snorted. "Sure." He jerked his head at a barrel behind him. "But it'll cost you more than the whiskey."

"Forget it."

He swept the bottle off the bar by the neck and the three of us retreated to one side and squatted on the ground. Wiley broke the seal and passed the bottle and each of us took a sip. Although I wasn't much of a hard-liquor drinker, there was no denying the smoothness of the Tennessee product.

The conversations resumed, although no one offered to talk to us. I felt uncomfortable but didn't sense any immediate threat from the men around us. The two men who had met us with the rifles were apparently explaining to some of the others that we were itinerant photographers, as heads turned in our direction and I could catch the drift of some of their words.

After the initial scrutiny, it became apparent that if we were to learn anything about this new camp we would have to take the initiative. We were pointedly ignored by the other men.

"I can't believe that all of them have been friends and acquaintances for a long time," Wiley remarked dryly to me, watching the men talking among themselves in twos and threes.

"Maybe they think if they pay us no mind we'll go away," I said, seeing the ebullient Burke being rebuffed in an attempt to strike up a conversation with an older miner sitting on the ground nearby. "Might be a better idea to just hang around a few days and start prospecting," I added. "Guess we shouldn't have expected them to jump to us with open arms."

"Men in mining camps are basically selfish," Wiley said. "But most of them, being strangers to each other and having a common interest, are forced to band together at least to form some kind of camp law for mutual protection against outlaws and claim jumpers."

"Maybe that's what they think we are — potential claim jumpers," I said. "I don't know why . . ." My thought was cut short by the rumbling of hooves, as several horses were pulled up short just outside the open fly of the saloon tent. Dust drifted into the lantern light, and all conversations stopped as the unseen riders dismounted amid grunts, the squeaking of leather, and the jingling of rowels.

Five men entered the tent, and an immediate, involuntary chill went over me at the sight of them. They were about as hard-eyed and cruel-looking a group as I had ever seen. Even though they were of only average height, they were lean and hard, with tied-down guns worn low, and they had the unshaven, dusty, red-eyed look of men who had been long on the trail. One man was bigger than the rest, more blocky than muscular. His big, square face was clean shaven and I saw that his hair was short as he swept off his hat and dropped it on the bar. His face bore an insolent, condescending look. But it was the eyes that really repelled me. They were blue, but somewhat close-set and piglike. As he turned and looked at the assembly, the eyes caught the light and reflected an opaque sheen.

"Gawd . . ." a miner near me breathed.

"Who is he?" I asked in an undertone.

"They call him 'Mad Dog.' "

Chapter 7

Then the recognition hit me. This was the man Major McCullough had told us about. This was the man who was feared and hated along the border almost as much as the raiding Apaches. All this had taken only the few seconds required for the five men to enter and walk up to the bar. The four gunmen with Mad Dog spread out so they could watch everyone in the saloon tent. But no one was making any move to oppose them. Even if we hadn't all been taken by surprise, I doubt that there would have been much resistance, judging from the looks on the miners' faces.

"Whiskey!" came the command from the one known as Mad Dog.

With an ill-concealed trembling hand, the wizened bartender reached into the wooden case for a bottle.

The outlaw twisted out the cork with a massive fist and turned up the bottle, taking three healthy swallows before lowering it and wiping the back of his hand across his mouth with a gasping grunt of satisfaction.

"Boys, I think we finally found us some decent whiskey," he boomed, holding the bottle at arm's length and examining the black and white label. His four cohorts grinned in anticipation, without taking their eyes off the rest of us, and did not move to drink until their leader gave the signal.

Mad Dog forced a mirthless grin. "I think just so's we'll all be more comfortable, everybody should toss his gun over here in a big pile. Alcohol and guns don't mix. Accidents *can* happen." He boomed out a short laugh.

Six-guns appeared in the hands of two of the outlaws. The motion of drawing was so fast I hardly saw it. The nervous miners needed no second invitation. Revolvers and bowie knives began falling onto the sandy soil at the feet of the outlaw leader. One poorly aimed toss struck his boot and bounced off, the hammer leaving a scar on the polished leather. The grin immediately disappeared from the big man's face. With a speed that belied his size, he covered the space that separated him from the miner and planted a vicious kick at the man's groin. The miner went down, rolling in agony on the ground, and the two remaining gunmen drew and covered us as several of the men moved to retaliate. Their instinctive reaction was stopped by the sharp clicks of hammers cocking. An ominous silence followed. Mad Dog was calmly pouring himself a drink in a cup he had washed in the bartender's expensive drinking water. The only indication of his violent attack was his slightly red face. He gulped down the shot of liquor and smacked his lips. "Damn good thing for you this isn't rotgut you're serving here," he said to the bartender.

"In fact, it's too good for a bunch o' dirt-grubbing prospectors." He turned to the youngest-looking of his henchmen. "Surefoot, get the rest o' that whiskey loaded up; we're takin' it with us."

The little bartender bristled as the lean outlaw brushed past him and yanked up the full case of Jack Daniels. "You can't do that! I've got a lot of money invested in that!"

"Shut up, old man," the young outlaw growled, hefting the case and starting outside toward the horses.

The other three gunmen, after making sure all visible weapons were collected in a pile, had relaxed enough to begin drinking. Burke still had his derringer tucked in the inside vest pocket, but dared not try for it.

One of the gunmen was not over five feet five and had long sideburns and ears that protruded from the sides of his head, presenting a ridiculous appearance. In an apparent attempt to compensate for his lack of height, he wore boots with extra-high heels and a tall sombrero. Another of the gunmen was a Mexican who sported new leather chaps and large rowels on his silver spurs, and affected a swagger when he moved. This man also had a lightning-fast left-handed draw and wore a dagger in a beaded sheath on his right hip.

Surefoot, the young, sallow-faced one, was still outside. The fourth gunman, a man I judged to be in his mid-thirties, was taller and had no particularly distinguishing features. He had the most intelligent face and was also the quietest.

Taken together, they were like some ludicrous desert monster that had suddenly come in out of the dark — but one that invited caution rather than laughter because of the danger of its deadly bite.

"What the hell are you starin' at?" Mad Dog demanded suddenly, glaring at one of the miners.

"Nothin'," the man mumbled, lowering his eyes.

"We been ridin' all day, and we need some grub," the leader declared after another quick shot of whiskey. "I'm sure you gents wouldn't mind rustlin' up some food for us." No one moved for a few seconds.

"Now!" he thundered, slamming the flat of his hand on the plank bar so hard that two tin cups jumped and slopped out their contents. Everyone in the tent jumped at the sudden outburst and two men started up to obey.

"Go with them," Mad Dog said to the quiet gunman, motioning with his head. The two miners and the outlaw disappeared into the night.

I glanced at Burke and Wiley. The redheaded Irishman did not seem the least bit afraid. On the contrary, his red face and bulging eyes made him appear about to explode with rage at what was taking place. I'm sure the only thing holding him back was his absolute helplessness in the situation. Any unarmed attack or any attempt to reach for his two-shot derringer would surely result in his death and maybe the killing of several others. Wiley's face was grim as he stared impassively at the gunmen who were drinking but were keeping their guns casually waving in our direction.

Where were the other men in this camp? What about the miners who were still in the stopes and on the hillsides, working by lantern light? Surely there were others who had retired to their own tents or dugouts and were cooking and eating their own suppers. Not everyone was in this saloon tent when Mad Dog and his men arrived. Apparently they had not heard or seen the new arrivals, or if they had, did not know anything was amiss. No fights had started and no noise or gunshots had disturbed the tranquillity of the night. The other prospectors in camp were apparently unaware of our plight.

And so we sat. The fresh smell of the cooling desert outside came to my nostrils. But there was also the smell of fear in the tense atmosphere in which we sat. The minutes dragged. The man who had been kicked in the groin was sitting up on the ground and moaning softly.

Finally, the two miners were escorted back in, carrying a tin pot of smoking beans, some corn-meal tortillas, and a small smoked ham, along with plates and forks. Mad Dog and his four men took some boxes to sit on, filled their plates, and dug in, ignoring us. The four henchmen had holstered their guns, evidently assuming they were safe from their cowed captives, and trusting to the quickness of their draws, should anyone walk in or make a move to escape or jump them. I was hoping the outlaws would finish, take whatever they wanted, and leave before someone tried to get heroic and foolishly go for them. It suddenly occurred to me that these outlaws were known to these miners. The man nearest me had even whispered the leader's name when they came in. Very likely these hardcase miners and frontiersmen had seen these outlaws in action before and were not about to oppose them.

But I had reckoned without the little barman. He was not about to let these men bully him and walk off with his stock of whiskey without a fight. He apparently had a short but heavy club stashed behind some crates near his chair in back of the plank bar where Mad Dog and two of his men sat eating. So quickly that I almost didn't see it, he snatched up the club and aimed a vicious swipe at the leader. The sudden movement caught the corner of my eye and apparently also caught Mad Dog's eye. The outlaw threw up his right arm at the last instant, but in time to catch the full force of the glancing blow. The club skipped off his forearm and bounced against Mad Dog's skull. He pitched over backward, kicking the plank bar up into the air as he did so. Several of us jumped for the other four outlaws at the same time. Looking back on it, our actions probably saved the bartender from being shot on the spot. But the gunmen were equal to the challenge. Colts appeared in their hands so fast that I never saw them draw. The deafening crash of a shot filled the tent, and one of the miners went down howling, shot in the foot. The rest of us stopped dead a few feet from the outlaws, suddenly realizing the folly of our move. In the few seconds it took for this to happen, the little barman was swinging the club in blind fury at the nearest outlaw, who happened to be the young kid. He caught him with a blow across the back before the quiet outlaw leaped on the little barman, slamming him to the ground and wrenching the club from his hands. The outlaw whipped the barrel of his Colt across the little man's head and left him stunned on the ground. This left only two men with guns on us but it was enough. The shot would bring the rest of the camp.

Mad Dog was slowly getting to his feet, spitting profanities and holding his right forearm. His piglike eyes were malevolent, and ignoring everyone else, he went for the stunned bartender who had assaulted him. While Burke, Wiley, the rest of the miners, and I looked on, he proceeded to aim kick after kick at the smaller man's ribs, all the time grunting and cursing and almost foaming at the mouth in rage.

I felt Burke stiffen beside me, and put my hand on his arm, just as one of the gunmen noticed the movement and swung his attention to us. "Don't get any heroic ideas," snarled the short man with the tall stetson. "Next time I won't shoot any-body in the foot."

The beating went on for several more seconds. The bartender was mercifully unconscious by now, and blood was oozing from his nose and mouth. With one last, vicious kick, Mad Dog apparently spent his rage, and the beating was over.

"Let's get out of here," he snapped at his men. The five of them melted toward the horses outside, the quiet one helping the young one who had been clubbed across the shoulders. In a matter of seconds, the five gunmen were in the saddle and galloping south in the darkness. As we swarmed out of the tent, one of the horsemen swung around in the saddle and fired two quick shots behind him. We scattered for cover, and several of us dove for our guns which still lay in a pile inside. A fusillade followed the fleeing outlaws, but if we hit anything, there was no indication of it.

By this time, there were shouts from the hillside as several more miners came running toward the commotion. But we paid little attention to their shouted questions.

"Get the horses and let's get after 'em!" There was a chorus of approval, and several of the men went running toward the picketed horses.

"Hold it! Hold it!" another voice yelled over the noise. "We'd never catch them in the dark. And if we did, they could ambush us anywhere out there in the moonlight." The men who were going for the horses slowed at his words. A couple of the less enthusiastic ones stopped and came back slowly toward the light of the saloon tent, as if they had been waiting for an excuse to drop the whole idea of pursuit.

"Let's see about Shorty," the same voice suggested, and all of us trooped back into the saloon, joined by a half-dozen miners fresh from their digs, who were grimed with sweat and dust. Spilled beans were all over the ground, and the yellow tortilla discs were scattered around.

Robert "Shorty" Anderson, the bartender, was conscious, but he had absorbed a fearful beating. After a quick examination by Wiley Jenkins and three or four of the miners, it appeared that the little man had at least three or four broken ribs, a probable concussion, and maybe other internal injuries.

"He's going to be stove up for a long time — maybe permanently," Wiley said quietly to me as the men gently lifted the bartender on a blanket and carried him out.

"That was a foolish move he made with that club," I answered as Burke joined us. "If he had let them alone, they probably would have left on their own shortly."

"Not without carrying off everything of value they could lay their hands on," a new voice said.

I looked up at a man standing close by who had overheard our conversation. It was the same man who had advocated restraint in the pursuit of the outlaws. He was of medium height but had a very regal, commanding air about him, fostered, no doubt, by the thick mane of silver hair and a stylish mustache and goatee to match. He appeared somewhat older and a little out of place in this group of rough miners.

"You were against going after them, and now you're saying that the bartender was right in trying to attack them, even though he nearly got himself killed?" Burke asked, his face rather flushed.

The white-haired man looked at Burke directly for the first time. "Not going after those men was only good sense, Mr. . . . ?"

"Burke. Paddy Burke."

"Mr. Burke. I'm Bill Hawkins. As for poor Anderson, he acted on his own, out of misguided bravery — or possibly frustration that his expensive stock of Jack Daniels whiskey was being taken. He certainly paid for his rash act; however, he did save the rest of us from being robbed."

"How do you know that?"

"Because these men have been here before," the cultured voice replied. "Less than a month ago. And they've hit some of the older mining towns as well. Take whatever they want, bully the population, and ride off. Mad Dog is getting quite a reputation in the territory."

"Why doesn't somebody put a stop to them?" Burke asked.

"A few have tried. Tried to rally support for a vigilance committee, tried to bushwhack them, tried to stand guard, tried to feed them poison."

"And?"

"Mad Dog and his boys must lead charmed lives. Nothing seems to work. About a half a dozen men who've tried to lay them out have turned up missing — just mysteriously disappeared — vanished . . . like when riding into town for supplies, out prospecting alone, going to the creek for water. One just vanished out of his own bed one night. Three of these men were later found — or rather, their bodies were found — mutilated — and not by any Indians. Two were impaled in a sitting position on sharpened stakes. One had been dragged naked behind a horse through a cactus patch. Two men tried to draw against them and were gunned down."

"Why doesn't the law take a hand?" Wiley wanted to know.

Hawkins laughed shortly. "How long have you been in this part of the territory? Law? There is no law out here except what a man carries on his hip."

"What about the soldiers at Fort Bowie or at the new Fort Huachuca, or Fort Thomas or Fort Apache?" Wiley asked.

"They're concerned with the Indian problem. Besides that, they don't have enough troopers to be everywhere at once. Outlaws — both Mex and gringos — are one of the hazards that go with this territory." He shrugged. "If a man can't take care of himself, he shouldn't be here."

"Doesn't look like the men in this camp are

very good at taking care of themselves," Wiley remarked.

"It will be some time before any government gets organized around here," Hawkins replied, unperturbed. "So far, there's no proof that Mad Dog's gang was involved in the killings and disappearances I mentioned. Only circumstantial evidence. And the shootings were fair fights, even if his men did provoke them. You noticed they were careful not to kill anyone here tonight."

"I'm sure the whole camp is grateful for that," Burke answered dryly.

"It's just easier to stay out of their way and let them have what they want. They haven't stolen any gold here, probably because so far our ore is too bulky and heavy and not rich enough for them to carry off. So far, there's no stamp mill close by. I think they know how far they can push us. Most of these miners are not interested in fighting; they came here to find minerals. Mad Dog's gang is like the other natural hazards of this area — heat, cactus, rattlesnakes, and scorpions — something to be ignored or avoided. Unless they get too deadly."

"Damn!" I shook my head in amazement. "Does everyone think like you do?"

"Enough of them. Most of these boys came west after the war. They've had their fill of fighting, on both sides, and they're looking to fill their pockets, not their graves. A lot of the Mexican peasants have survived banditos and revolutions south of the border just that way for years. Besides," he said, his face taking on a hard look, "there will be another time for us — when the odds are better."

"Where did they take the bartender?" Wiley asked, suddenly changing the subject.

"Probably up to his tent to take care of him."

"If he dies, Mad Dog's got a provable murder on his head."

"Not necessarily. Shorty attacked him first. There are some slick lawyers in Tucson."

"I can't believe my ears. Let's get out of here," Burke said disgustedly. He stalked out of the tent, his normally ruddy complexion even redder.

Wiley and I followed him out into the cool night.

Chapter 8

"All right, now, let me get a shot of you standing up by the windlass with a pick or shovel in your hand," Burke directed Bob Welch, the short miner who had greeted our arrival with a Winchester. The man had shown up at our wagon with his partner just after breakfast in clean overalls and flannel shirt, shaved and ready to freeze his image on a glass negative for posterity.

The mid-morning sun and the clear air in the Dos Cabezas Mountains made a perfect setting for picture-taking, and almost made Mad Dog's raid of the night before seem like a bad dream. The short miner's partner, Charley Singleton, posed on the other side of the windlass frame with his hand on the crank. Wiley and I had helped pack the dark tent, the boxes containing the glass plates, and bottles of chemicals from Burke's wagon up to the site of the miner's diggings. Burke, himself, had shouldered the seventy-pound camera and tripod and climbed the steep hills to get here.

It was a good morning to be alive — a morning designed to make a man forget his troubles. But the fresh air and exercise was rapidly burning up the substantial breakfast of flapjacks, bacon, and coffee I had put away just after sunrise.

As I watched the redhead get set up for the exposure, I couldn't help thinking of the events of the night before. The two miners had not mentioned the episode and the other men in camp were going about their business as if the whole thing had been a minor incident not worthy of discussion. Their attitude seemed to be: as long as the outlaws are gone, they are best forgotten. Everyone was back at the primary business of finding new lodes and hacking and blasting mineral-bearing ore out of existing claims.

I had not seen the white-haired man named Hawkins this morning. However, he had not struck me as the type who would be up at daybreak straining himself with manual labor. That being the case, I couldn't imagine what he was doing here; this was certainly not anywhere close to being a town yet.

"Okay, gents, hold it right there and look this way," the photographer said, pulling his head from under the drape behind the camera and reaching around to uncap the brass tube that contained the lens. His habitually disheveled red hair almost glowed in the warm sunlight. Burke owned a hat, but seldom wore it, he told me, except in cold or rainy weather, or "unless the sun is about to fry my brains."

The photography session was over, and several other men, who had been watching curiously, came forward to inquire about having their own likenesses duplicated.

With exposed plate in hand, Burke was just

entering the dark tent we had set up nearby to develop the photo, when one of the miners, looking south toward the camp on the slope below, remarked, "There goes poor Shorty and Walker."

A wagon was pulling out of camp and rolling down the faint trail toward the ford. A slight figure was stretched full-length on blankets in back, and the man who had been shot in the foot sat propped in the wagon bed beside him, with his bandaged foot elevated on a roll of canvas tenting. Even though the team was moving slowly, the unsprung wagon jolted over ruts and rocks as it moved alongside the dry streambed.

"Where are they going?" Wiley asked.

"Probably to Fort Bowie," the tall man with the slicked-down hair replied. "The nearest doctor. That's Tom Jernigan driving. He and Brad Smith take a load of ore to Tucson about every two weeks and bring back supplies and mail. But they carry two armed guards with them on those trips."

"Do you have to send your ore all the way to Tucson?"

"There's no closer stamp mill that we have access to. Exceptin' this one's got a big wheel rather than just draggin' a big rock. There — you can see it working right over there."

We followed his pointing finger and saw a mule plodding around in a circle, attached to a pole about eight feet long, which pivoted around a center point. Attached to this pole was a large stone mill wheel — similar to one used by a grist mill — rolling over and crushing chunks of ore spread in a circular track paved with flat stones.

"Pretty crude," Wiley remarked.

"Yeah, but it's better than nothin'. They carted that mill wheel from Tucson. That keeps the pack mules or wagons from haulin' a lot of worthless rock. Only the best stuff is sent on to the mill. They're saving the rest o' the ore 'til we get a stamp mill and reduction works somewhere closer. It's only a matter o' time. The main problem is lack o' water. I hear some men are setting up a stamp mill on the San Pedro about forty miles from here. It's a long way, but it's still only half as far as Tucson."

"How long has this camp been here?" I asked, taking advantage of the miner's expansive mood. He didn't seem to be in a hurry to go to work.

"The Casey brothers were actually the first ones to find mineral here about three months ago. That's their dugout you passed coming up here. A couple o' old bachelors who are as strange as they come. They didn't hit any mother lode, but the quartz looks good. The word got out, and the rest of us been driftin' in here a few at a time during the past few weeks. Hope there's no big rush 'til we get ours. We really need an assay on what we've found so far, but everybody knows the deeper ya go, the wider the pay streak. If we can get down far enough into this-here outcropping . . ."

"If you don't quit yapping and come help me,

114

we'll be settin' at this same level at this time next month," his taciturn partner interrupted irritably. From the look on Bob Welch's face, I guessed he had cut off his voluble partner more to keep him from revealing further details of their claim than to get him working.

Burke was still in his "dark tent," a small, one-man affair he carted around with him whenever he wasn't close to the darkroom in the wagon. The windowless dark tent had a yellow lining that let in just enough light for Burke to see what he was doing. The lining let in colored light only. The light-sensitive collodian plates reacted only to blue light. These airless tents were very hot to work in, especially in the summer, and most especially in the desert summer, Burke had told me. He had to work fast to keep salty perspiration on his face and arms from dripping into the chemical baths.

Just then he loosened the flap and backed out of the tent, handing me three glass plate negatives he had just developed. I laid them out carefully to dry before slipping them into the slotted wooden holders in the wooden box for packing. We helped him put away the bottles of chemicals, fold up the tripod and tent, and pack all the gear for the trip down the mountain to his wagon.

Seeing the New Yorker at work recording these scenes reminded me with a start that I needed to be taking some notes in preparation for writing up my articles for *Harper's Weekly*.

115

My job was to report on the new strikes and mines being developed in the southern Arizona Territory. So far, I had filed only one short article by telegraph from Fort Bowie. And it had taken some powerful persuasion for me to talk Major McCullough into letting me use the new military telegraph to file my article. My story had contained an account of the fight with the Apaches and the mysterious stranger who had given us refuge in the abandoned mine. It also included a brief description of Fort Bowie and Apache Pass — places I thought would interest my eastern readers and keep the editor on the string for more.

"While Burke is recouping his fortunes with his camera, do you want to take a shot at a little prospecting, ourselves?" Wiley inquired of me after we had helped set up Paddy's equipment for another picture-making session in the makeshift camp at the base of the slopes.

"I don't know," I replied dubiously, glancing up at the Dos Cabezas Mountains behind us. "It's one thing to do a little panning and placer mining in the Black Hills, but this looks like real work. The whole mountain range looks like it's solid granite and quartz. Besides, we haven't got any tools, and I doubt if we'll find any for sale among this group."

"Work?" he grimaced. "That word makes my back hurt. I'm talking about poking around farther back in those mountains — maybe knock off a chunk or two of quartz with a prospector's hammer. Nothing strenuous. Let's go back to the wagon and get Burke's field glasses. I want to take a closer look at some of the outcroppings a mile or two to the west of here, toward the end of this range. The way those big ledges are tilted and from the color of them, they may show some promise."

I considered the idea. It sure beat hanging around camp the rest of the day with nothing to do while Burke printed up the glass negatives in his wagon.

"Sure, why not?"

"Good. You rustle us up some hardtack and jerky to take along for lunch, and I'll see if I can round up a pick or a hammer of some kind."

In less than an hour we were on our way. It was almost like a picnic. The air was crystal clear and suffused with golden sunshine that drove the October temperature into the eighties. As we walked our horses west along the base of the mountains, the air was mildly fragrant with the fresh scent of creosote bushes and sage. A hawk soared high on the updrafts of the warm midday air, veering gracefully against the deep blue of the sky. There was no place in the world I would have preferred to be at that moment.

That didn't mean I was totally relaxed. Constant vigilance was the price of survival in this part of the country. We both carried our loaded rifles across the pommels of our saddles. Wiley had Burke's Henry rifle, and both of us wore our Colts. I was even wearing a sheathed bowie knife

— probably, I had to admit, as much for digging and prying up loose rocks as for protection. Any number of Apaches could be concealed among the large mesquite trees through which we were threading our way, so an ambush was entirely possible. Somehow I felt that we were in little danger from any gang of outlaws such as Mad Dog. They were probably miles from here by now. It was the Apaches who presented the threat, no matter how peaceful the scene.

When we neared the end of the range about three miles from the Dos Cabezas camp, Wiley pulled up and studied the formations above us through Burke's field glasses.

"There," he pointed. "That's what I was looking at earlier. See those big outcroppings where the ledges are tilted out of the ground?"

"Let's take a look."

We dismounted, hobbled our horses, loosened their cinches slightly, and slipped their bits to allow them to graze on the nutritious gramma grass that grew thickly in the area. Then, taking our rifles, canteens, and a small pack containing our lunch and a couple of small picks, we started our climb.

An hour later we reached the outcroppings, gigantic upthrust slabs of rock tilted and bucked up at a forty-five-degree angle. Looking back as we paused to catch our breath and drink from our canteens, we could see the tiny cluster of tents and tiny adobe buildings that comprised the camp of Dos Cabezas. To the south, a mile or two away, was a line of low, undulating hills that paralleled the much larger Dos Cabezas Mountains where we stood. It was almost as if those few small hills had been put there to form the wide, shallow valley at our feet, which was thickly covered with desert growth of mesquite, creosote bush, Joshua trees, spiky yucca, cholla, and a variety of other desert plants I wasn't familiar with. We could see the tracings of several small watercourses cutting their sandy way down out of the mountains and across the valley to disappear somewhere near the low hills that formed the far side of the valley. Beyond was the vast, flat grassland some of the men had referred to as the Sulphur Springs Valley. Farther to the south and east, the Chiricahuas reared their foreboding bulk against the sky. The stage road snaked its way along the base of the mountain chain, disappearing toward Apache Pass to the east.

Far to the right and south of our short valley, the sun glistened off what appeared to be a flat sheet of water.

"Is that a mirage?" I asked, pointing. Wiley shifted the small pack on his back and stared in that direction for a few seconds.

"Naw. Must be that dry lake bed the boys in camp were talking about. Except it's not dry now. There's been a lot of rain around here last month, I hear. The lake'll be dry again in a few weeks." The squinted eyes under his brim swept around at the panorama of the Dos Cabezas.

Everything in this part of the country — mesas, mountains, and deserts — was on such a massive scale that I had trouble trying to assimilate it all. Sizes and distances were so vast that mere human beings shrank to antlike proportions by comparison.

I looked down to be sure our horses were grazing below us, unmolested.

"Let's go."

We climbed and stumbled our way over the jumble of rocks, loose shale, and boulders that were thickly laced with cactus plants of every description. The pitch of the slope was steep and the going incredibly rugged. My good and only pair of boots were being scuffed and scarred badly by the rocks and spines of Spanish bayonet, catclaw, and prickly pear — all aptly named. It was nearly impossible to climb across the steep face of the hill by using our hands to steady ourselves.

"There's a hunk o' quartz sticking out up here, if I can just get to it," Wiley panted.

The hill began to level out as we neared the top, where a massive slab of rock jutted up from the ridgetop. The slab projected another thirty or forty feet above us. The sides of it were cracked and seamed and weathered by the eons of wind and rain and shiftings of the earth.

I was about ten feet behind him as he rounded the narrow ledge at the base of the slab.

"Yeeoow!" Wiley yelled and jumped sideways. His foot hit the loose rocks and he cartwheeled down the steep slope to our left, into a thick patch of cactus some fifteen feet below.

With his anguished wail in my ears, I caught a movement on the ledge where he had been standing. A sunning rattlesnake was uncoiling and beginning to slide away out of sight around the slab.

"Oh, God! Matt! Ohh!"

I took one last, quick look toward the spot where the snake had disappeared, and then began a careful descent of the slope.

"Anything busted?" I yelled.

"I can't move!"

"Where're you hurt?"

"Everywhere!" came the cry.

In a few seconds I was crouching at his side as he tried to struggle to a sitting position. Every movement brought gasps of pain. His shirt was shredded and he was bleeding from dozens of wounds from the razor-sharp yucca. Trickles of blood were running from cuts and scratches on his face and in his scalp. I looked quickly at his eyes. They were unhurt.

"No bones broken?" I asked again.

He forced a grin. "I can't move enough to tell."

Thousands of tiny barbs furred his left pants leg and shoulder, the results of an encounter with a cholla on the way down. I took his arm and eased him into a sitting position. He bit his lips to keep from crying out as the tiny spines buried themselves deeper in his flesh. He moved tentatively.

"Nothing's broken, I guess."

"Good. We're halfway there." I tried to sound cheerful as I took my bowie knife and carefully slit away the remains of his tattered shirt. With any luck at all, many of the spines would come away with the cloth.

"You're mighty lucky. You could've impaled yourself on that big Spanish bayonet."

"I shoulda taken my chances with that rattler." He laughed dryly. "Maybe his fangs wouldn't have penetrated my boot."

"Instinct," I said. "Glad to see your reflexes are still okay." My bowie knife was still working. "Let's get these pants off, too. Then we'll see about getting you down this mountain in your longhandles and your boots."

Chapter 9

Paddy Burke and I worked on Wiley's anatomy off and on for three days before we got most of the stickers out of it. The larger thorns were no problem: it was the hundreds of tiny, translucent, almost invisible spines that proved the most difficult. Wiley was living testimony that they could certainly be felt, even if not seen.

"Every damn thing in the territory has thorns, fangs, or stingers," Wiley gritted through clenched teeth as he lay facedown on the table in Burke's wagon while we probed his posterior one more time. "The Apaches fit right in here. They're as hostile as the environment."

Some of the smallest barbs we never did get.

"They'll just have to fester and work their way out, or stay in there," Burke commented when we had finally done all we could. We had washed and sterilized all his cuts and bandaged a couple of the worst ones on his upper left arm.

"Did that cool your enthusiasm for prospecting?"

"Well, if I do any more, it'll be someplace where I don't have to do any climbing."

"You may be interested in moving on, then," Burke said. "I've cleaned up about all the picture-making business there is in this camp."

"Good idea." Wiley nodded. "They seem to think my fall into that cactus was a big joke. I should be able to sit a horse in a day or two."

"Suits me," I agreed quickly. I was getting bored already. I felt it was time to move on to other new camps to the south and west we had heard talk of. Some promising ore was being taken by a few of the prospectors on the slopes of the Dos Cabezas, but no bonanzas were being struck as yet.

I had interviewed about a dozen of the miners, and had written up another short article for *Harper's*. But I had no means of transmitting the story until I could get somewhere to mail it or send it over the telegraph. I had considered trying to flag down an eastbound mail stage to send my article east that way. But only one celerity stage had appeared in the few days we had been at Dos Cabezas, and it went barreling west before dawn one morning, without stopping. Two stages per week each way from Tucson through Apache Pass to Mesilla, New Mexico Territory, and on to El Paso was supposed to be the schedule. But the raiding Apaches were playing havoc with any kind of timetable. To be sure my article got through, I decided to hold on to it until I could post it at some safer, more civilized place.

There was little or no organized defense of the Dos Cabezas camp. Even though the threat of Apaches was ever-present, and the episode of Mad Dog and his men proved how vulnerable this camp was, the miners and prospectors apparently still felt that each man, partnership, or group of men should go it alone. Except for the white-bearded Hawkins, I had encountered no lone prospectors. Each man there had at least one partner, and the largest group was composed of six men. Each of these units looked out for itself and stood guard over its own claims. Each was here separately to claw at the earth, to force it, or coax it, to give up its precious metals as quickly as possible. Then, if the ore were widely dispersed or low-grade, or if it required the investment of much capital, machinery, and labor to extract what gold and silver there was, most of these men would sell out for what they could get from any potential buyer and move on to new diggings. The pattern had been the same in the Black Hills and in Colorado. These prospectors were the pioneers of the mining industry, and most of them would probably die with little more than they started with. Only a few of them would be persistent, smart, or lucky enough to become wealthy.

"What did you ever find out about that man Hawkins?" Wiley asked, interrupting my reverie as he finished putting on his clothes and stepped down from the wagon so Burke could use the darkroom inside. I was sitting on a box in the shade, packing my pipe.

"Nobody seems to know much about him. He's been here a few weeks, but he's not prospecting. He's been looking over some of the

125

claims, and rumor has it that he represents some big money interests from San Francisco and is looking for some promising properties if any of these claims turn out to be such. But apparently he himself hasn't said much to anybody. Pretty close-mouthed."

"Yeah. He looks the part." Wiley nodded. He leaned against the wagon, not daring to entrust his tender rear end to the hard ground or the wagon tongue.

I raked a match across a rock and applied it to my pipe bowl. In the few seconds of silence in which I puffed it into life, I caught the faint jingle of trace chains and glanced toward the stage road. A team of mules hauling a wagon was in view, and the rig was leading a light cloud of dust as it wound up the faint, curving track from the stage road to the camp. The rig disappeared into a dry wash, only to reappear a few minutes later, much closer, and I recognized the driver.

"That's the man who hauled Shorty and that wounded miner to Fort Bowie," Wiley said, voicing my thoughts.

The wagon rolled on past our campsite and finally drew up in the middle of the camp, a few hundred feet farther on.

Wiley and I followed on foot and came up to the wagon just as the driver, who had stepped down, was being greeted by a half-dozen men who weren't up working on their claims.

"Sutler wouldn't sell me more'n a hundred pounds o' these beans," the driver said, moving around to the tailgate.

"T'hell with that, Tom. How's Shorty?"

The driver paused, his hand on the edge of the rough wood. "Well, boys, he's still alive, but he's in bad shape. That's the reason I stayed over there so long. Thought maybe I'd just wait and bring his body back. The doc's done all he can for him, but he's still not sure if he's gonna make it. He's rallied some, but Doc says he's got internal injuries. It's touch and go, but I finally had to get on back. My partner's up there doin' all the work hisself. Reckon I'd better get up there and help him."

"Any Injun sign?" somebody asked.

"Nary a bit. I tried to travel the pass before dawn or just after dark. I hear the Apaches won't attack in the dark. But it's pure hell tryin' to go through those canyons and find the fort, with no light but the moon."

Several of us were lending a hand unloading the supplies from the wagon as Tom Jernigan talked.

"By the way, where's that photographer?" the driver asked, looking around. "The Doc said to tell him that his apprentice still can't travel. He'll have to stay there at least another two weeks. Some problem with infection."

"We'll tell him," I answered. "He's back in his darkroom."

Jernigan nodded. "Just stash this stuff in my tent, boys, until I can settle up with the ones who ordered it." The driver took off his hat and wiped a sleeve across his forehead. "You know, the damnedest thing happened while I was there. The night after I arrived, somebody left a small bag of gold for Shorty."

"Who did it?"

"Nobody knows. Somebody just slipped into the fort past the sentry during the night and flung a small buckskin poke of gold right through the window of the commanding officer's bedroom. Scared hell out of his wife and made the major fightin' mad, since it busted out a good pane o' glass."

"Gold? You mean gold coins?"

"No, but it might as well have been. It was several small chunks of sponge gold, pure as I've ever seen it, with only about a third of it composed of quartz. I got a good look at it when Major McCullough brought it down to the post hospital, before he locked it up in his safe. Musta been worth at least a thousand. Besides the gold, the poke had a little piece of paper in it with two words, 'Shorty Anderson,' printed on it in pencil. The major didn't even know who Shorty was until he got to askin' around. You boys know anything about it?"

The half-dozen men glanced at each other blankly.

"Did the gold look like it came from around these parts?" one of them asked.

"Sure looked like it to me. But this came from a much purer vein than anybody in the camp has struck. 'Most all the other minerals except the white quartz had been leached out of it, leaving the gold looking like hard sponge."

"Did Shorty have a nest egg we didn't know about — maybe a silent partner who threw that gold in?"

Again, everybody was at a loss for answers.

"If he did any prospecting, I sure didn't know of it. He just rolled in here by hisself about a month ago with a tent and a few cases of whiskey on his wagon and set up a saloon. I heard he came over from San Diego."

We had finished stacking the few sacks and boxes in Jernigan's tent and two of the men were unharnessing the team.

"If Shorty dies, somebody'll have to find out if he's got family somewhere to send that gold to."

"But if he lives, that'll take care of things pretty well until he gets back on his feet."

I shook my head as Wiley and I walked off. "Christmas about two months early."

"Shorty Anderson's apparently a big favorite with these boys. Guess it probably couldn't have happened to a better fella. What say we get some lunch? My stomach is rumbling."

"Go ahead. I want to see Bill Hawkins for a few minutes."

I found the white-haired Hawkins relaxing on a cot in his tent, reading a book. He put it aside and sat up as I came in.

"Sure, I've seen him around here off and on since I came to this camp," he told me when I asked him about the elusive stranger who had saved us in Apache Pass. "The other men tell me he's been showing up periodically since the first prospectors came a few months ago. Unusual man. He never says much, never prospects. He does a few odd jobs for something to eat, or for tips. Looks sick all the time. Pale. I've heard that he's an alcoholic, although I've never seen him drunk around here. All the men like him. He's like an old stray dog — everybody's friend. I'd guess he's probably one of those men who can't live in society for some reason. Shady past, maybe."

The next day, shortly before sundown, we pulled out for the west, Wiley and Burke riding the converted ambulance, trailing one horse behind, while I was horseback and scouted about a half-mile ahead on the stage road. Night travel was safer and the stage road was easier to follow, especially on a clear night with a half-moon showing. I knew there was no way, even in daylight, that I would see any Apaches, if they didn't want to be seen. The most I could hope for, in the case of a surprise ambush, was that Paddy and Wiley would have enough warning to defend themselves. Our best insurance, though, was the cover of night, when the superstitious Apaches apparently would not fight.

Our goal before daylight was the fantastic jumble of rocks that Wiley told us lay about thirty miles to the southwest. Here we hoped to make camp near the road, in the protection of these giant boulders, and rest during the day.

During the afternoon, white, cottony, summerlike clouds had built up over the mountains. But today, instead of dissipating, as they usually did, the clouds began to mass into tall thunderheads, their bases solidifying and turning dark. As we packed our meager gear and said our good-byes to the men we had met at the camp, jagged forks of lightning stabbed out from the bases of these black clouds, followed by the faint rumblings of thunder a few seconds later. Gray veils of rain swept across some of the distant peaks and valleys of the Chiricahuas to the southeast of us. As the sun dropped over the western horizon and the light began to fail quickly, I looked back over my shoulder to see the rain spreading over the Apache Pass area and the sky filling rapidly with clouds behind us, even though there was little wind.

Scouting ahead by myself got lonesome, so I rode back to the wagon before twilight turned into complete darkness.

"Looks like we might be in for a nasty night," I said, pulling my mount alongside the right-hand driver's side. "How about handing my poncho out, Wiley?"

When the rain gear was settled over my head, covering my thighs and the saddle as well, I said, "If you don't see me about every fifteen or twenty minutes, pull up and turn this rig around and get back to Dos Cabezas as fast as these mules can take you, 'cause something will

131

have happened to me."

I tugged my hat down as a sudden gust of wind kicked up dust from the road and a few drops of rain hit my face. I waved my hand and kicked my horse into a canter to move out ahead. With no moon or stars to light the unfamiliar stage road, I'd be able to see virtually nothing. I'd be lucky to stay on the faint road at all, even though the old Butterfield stage road had been well-worn over the years. The wind began to kick up as the darkening sky filled with approaching rain clouds. A sudden flash of lightning lit up the landscape brilliantly for a second, and then everything was plunged into blackness again and I was temporarily blinded, as a crash of thunder heralded the splattering of rain. I hunched down and flipped the front of my poncho partially over my Winchester, which I carried fully loaded across the pommel of my saddle. I also carried my Colt strapped to my waist under the poncho and my bowie knife in a sheath on my left side. Yet, as well armed as I was, I still felt like a helpless decoy. My only hope was that no one else would be foolish enough to be out in this storm. Another flash of lightning lit up the road as it dipped and curved, generally following the base of the Dos Cabezas before bending left out of our short valley toward the wide, shallow lake a few miles ahead. Each time the lightning etched everything in brilliant detail for a second, I tried to freeze the image of the scene on my mind's eye until the next flash showed me the way. I only hoped no one else was watching this road and seeing me riding down the middle of it.

The lightning and thunder increased as the storm front came directly over us. The rain turned into a steady downpour that soaked through my hat, and the rivulets of water ran off the poncho into my boots. As the night wore on, I had to estimate the time intervals to swing back toward the wagon and give Wiley and Paddy a quick view of me before moving the better part of a mile in front. As the rain continued, the runoff from the nearby mountains caused some streams to flow over the low spots in the road. Most of these I saw before my mount was into them, but my horse came up short and refused to cross one such stream. I hoped he didn't sense a flash flood rushing down on us. I couldn't see or hear anything over the storm. I dismounted and, feeling my way with my feet, led him into the swiftly flowing, unseen water. The stream was no more than knee-deep, but the current was so swift it almost took my feet from under me. The wet-weather ford was about ten yards across, and when I had waded up the far side, I waited for the ambulance to approach to tell them the crossing was safe.

As I stood there, feeling increasingly uncomfortable and tired, with water trickling down my neck, I wished I was rolled into my dry bedroll sound asleep. But I wished even more that the rain would stop. Somewhere up ahead the road

133

might be impassable from flash flooding. But we had started, so I saw no point in stopping unless or until we had to.

The wagon came up slowly to the ford, and Burke drew the mules to a halt.

"Burke!" I called out, suddenly realizing he couldn't see me. "Bring it on across; it's only about two feet deep. The bottom's solid, but take it easy. It's pretty swift."

The photographer brought the wagon through without mishap, and pulled up beside me.

"What time is it?" I asked.

Wiley pulled out his watch and struck a match under the overhang of the wagon roof to look at it.

"A little after ten."

The way I felt, I just knew it had to be long after midnight. I waved my acknowledgment and pulled my horse's head around to lead out once more.

In less than twenty minutes I was stopped by an instant river that looked uncrossable. In the darkness, I couldn't tell how wide it was, but I guessed it to be more than a hundred feet. My horse absolutely refused to enter the rushing torrent, so I dismounted and, gripping his bridle in one hand and my rifle in the other, started to lead him. He snorted and jerked his head back in fear. Maybe he instinctively knows more than I do, I thought. But he finally began to step forward. I had waded no more than three steps into the water, when both feet slipped out from under me as the muddy bottom of the desert wash dropped off sharply. The only thing that kept me from going completely under was my hold on my horse's bridle.

"Whoa, boy! Whoa!" I gasped. The sudden jerk on my horse's head caused him to stumble sideways, as his forelegs slid into deeper water. But, between the two of us, we clawed our way back to solid ground. "Atta boy. Easy now," I panted, struggling to my feet and patting him on the neck. "You had enough sense for the both of us. I shoulda listened to you."

I was soaked to the skin. As I stood there catching my breath, it seemed the roar of the water in the normally dry desert wash was growing louder by the second. I knew there would be no crossing this wild water for the next few hours, even if the rain stopped now, which it showed no sign of doing. I was thoroughly chilled and shivering in my soggy clothes, so I walked my horse back up the road to get my blood circulating.

I waved down the ambulance a minute later and explained the situation.

"All we can do is pull 'er off the road and hole up for the night. Maybe it'll look better to-morrow, or we might be able to find a ford in the daylight," Burke yelled above the roar. "I just hate to take a chance on being caught in the open like I was in Apache Pass. Might not be so lucky the second time."

I knew from that first experience that this was

one Irishman who was afraid of nothing; his concern was merely logical — not fearful. I didn't answer for a moment as I considered the alternatives. Rain was pouring in sheets off the front overhang of the wagon.

"We're nearing the west end of the Dos Cabezas," Wiley offered. "We won't be too obvious if we camp in some o' those heavy stands of big mesquite."

"Sounds good to me," I nodded, the rain sluicing off my hat brim. "Stay here a few minutes and I'll ride up that way and scout it out."

Roughly an hour later, the converted ambulance had jolted over the last bump, and Burke pulled the mules up in a dense stand of mesquite trees and set the brake. As near as we could tell, we were safe enough, on higher ground, from any flood threat. I got the mules unhitched, since I was already soaking wet. I strung a picket line from the wagon to the thick trunk of a mesquite, and fed them some of the grain we had brought along. They would be safe enough, as long as one of us stood guard in the partial shelter of the driver's seat. We could take turns on watch since there was barely room for two sleepers inside the wagon, what with the interior of the old army ambulance being converted to a darkroom and crammed with cameras, boxes of glass plates, bottles of chemicals, tripods, coils of rope, and other gear.

When we had gotten situated, Wiley volunteered to stand the first watch. "I haven't been driving or out scouting in the rain," he reasoned, taking Burke's still-dry Henry rifle.

I stripped off my drenched clothing and rolled gratefully into my blankets on the floorboards, and Burke stretched out on the narrow work table which was doing double duty as his bunk. With my fatigue, the warmth of the blankets, and the soothing sound of the rain on the roof, I was asleep almost at once.

"Matt! Matt! Wake up!"

"My watch already?" I groaned sleepily in response to Wiley's urgent whisper. I felt as if I had just closed my eyes.

"No. No. I heard some kind of wailing sound over the noise of the storm."

"Wailing?" I rolled over on one elbow and rubbed my eyes. What kind of raving was this? Was Wiley's imagination getting the better of him? It really wasn't like him. He wasn't usually that jumpy. Probably the moaning of the wind through the mesquite and palo verde.

But I rolled out of my blankets, shivering in my long johns, and stepped carefully past the sleeping Burke to the front seat of the wagon.

"Listen."

I strained my ears as the mist blew against my face. Nothing. Then, above the wind and the thrashing of the wet foliage, came some kind of unusual noise. Then it was gone. But it came again, this time more distinctly. I listened intently. The sound rose and fell.

"That's somebody singing!" Wiley declared.

Chapter 10

Wiley and I looked at each other, even though I could not see his face. I was incredulous. There couldn't be anyone out here, especially on a night like this. And singing? It was impossible — some trick of the keening wind blowing down from the rocks. The eerie noise made the hair rise on the back of my neck.

"You reckon we accidentally parked this thing near somebody's camp?" Wiley asked. The wavering sound tailed away and was swallowed up in a crash of thunder.

"Probably a bobcat or mountain lion," I suggested, doubting my words even as I spoke. "Maybe even a coyote."

"I don't think so," Wiley sounded certain.

"Okay. Let me get my clothes on; we'll check it out."

I rummaged in my duffle for some dry clothes, pulled on my cold, soggy boots and hat, and shrugged into my poncho before waking up Burke. I briefly explained where we were going. "If you don't hear from us in about thirty minutes, better come looking."

Burke nodded and reached for his gunbelt.

Wiley had the Henry and I took my Winchester. We stepped into the darkness and checked the horses and mules on our picket line. They stood with heads down, and streaming water, mutely enduring the storm.

Wiley motioned with his arm, and we cautiously stepped between the big mesquite trees, their wet branches brushing us. I glanced behind me to be sure I knew where the wagon was, so I could find my way back. With no stars or moon, it would be easy to get turned around.

The sandy soil made for good footing. The sound started again. A gust of wind carried the noise away from us for a few seconds, but the sound returned. No doubt about it — it was a human voice. Snatches of the tune even began to sound familiar as we got closer, holding our rifles ready. Of all things, it sounded like a man singing, or attempting to sing, "Tenting Tonight on the Old Camp Ground." We had hardly gone more than fifty yards through the thick desert growth when suddenly we stumbled into an open area and stopped short at the sight of a small square of yellow light shining from a window. The voice of the singer wavered to a stop and ended in a fit of coughing.

A white flash of electricity stabbed the ground a few yards away and I recoiled, half blinded, my throat constricting in sudden fear. The sizzle of the close lightning discharge was immediately drowned in a ground-shaking clap of thunder.

When my numbed senses began to clear, I found myself on hands and knees in sand and mud, my rifle still gripped in one hand, as the rain sluiced down over me in sheets. I staggered to my feet and looked for Wiley, but saw only the yellow square of light in the blackness. Then another flash of lightning illuminated a small stone cabin. I caught sight of Wiley ahead of me. We moved forward slowly, the sound of our approach masked by the storm, and slid up to each side of the glassless window. Removing my hat, I eased my right eye cautiously around the edge of the opening and looked inside.

The sudden brightness blinded me for a second or two, but then things came quickly into focus. The silhouette of a man was not eight feet from me. I jerked my head back before I realized he was seated with his back to me and looking toward the blazing hearth against the opposite wall. I looked again. The wavering light cast by the leaping flames showed the room to be empty except for the hulking figure sitting cross-legged in the center. His saddle lay next to him. Even as I looked, the man cleared his throat and tilted a small stoneware jug to his mouth and took a short pull. His shaggy hair fell over his collar and he was roughly dressed in a canvas coat, but I could tell little else about him. The flames in the stone fireplace alternately flared up and were beaten back with a hissing of rain as the wind gusted down or sucked the draft up the chimney. There was a wooden door on the south side of the room which was hanging askew from one leather hinge. It only partially filled the doorway, and water was running down the inside, staining the rough wood. If the man was armed, it wasn't obvious. I didn't see a long gun, but he very likely had a belt gun under his coat. No man in his right mind went unarmed in this country. I pulled my head back and put on my hat. Wiping a hand across my wet face, I stared past the lighted opening at Wiley. He had seen what was inside and looked as mystified as I felt. I wasn't leaving here until I found out who this man was and what he was doing sitting alone, drinking and singing in a cabin in a desert thunderstorm in the middle of Apache country.

I motioned silently to Wiley. He crouched under the window and we ducked around the corner toward the door. On signal, Wiley kicked the sagging door and it flew inward.

Before the door even stopped moving, I was inside, covering the room with my Winchester.

The man seated on the floor jerked around in our direction and instantly rolled over on his back, howling like a coyote. The howls tailed off into maniacal laughter that caused chills to run up my back. I glanced quickly at Wiley who was inside staring at this apparition. Then the howling began again. The man was either completely drunk, or crazy, or having some sort of seizure. The howling was eerie in the flickering firelight of the lonely cabin. I had instinctively backed up toward the open doorway, still covering the thrashing figure on the sandy floor.

Then the howling and laughter stopped abruptly, as the bearded, shaggy man rolled on his

141

back where he could get a good look at us. "Aw, shit!" He started to say something else as he slowly pushed himself to a sitting position, but the words were choked off in a paroxysm of coughing. He coughed and gagged for a good half-minute before he spat into a corner and drew a deep breath. His face was flushed in the firelight.

"You boys gave me quite a start. Thought it was the Apaches."

There was something familiar about the man's voice, and as I moved around toward the fireplace, he turned his face toward me and the light. Then the shock of recognition hit me, and I lowered my rifle. Peering out of the tangle of hair and beard was the face of the stranger who had saved us from the war party by hiding us in the mine tunnel near Fort Bowie.

"What the hell you doing here?" Wiley managed to say, as the stranger retrieved his stoneware bottle and settled the phlegm in his throat with another long swallow.

I lowered the hammer of my Winchester and leaned it in the corner next to the hearth and then moved closer to the fire to warm my wet, chilled body. A three-foot-high stack of dry wood and brush was piled in a far corner.

"I'm keepin' the outside of me dry and the inside wet," retorted the stranger, glaring at us. "You're two o' them that had the set-to with the Indians in Apache Pass."

"That's right," Wiley replied, removing his hat and shaking the water from it. I stepped over to the door and slid and propped it back in place as the gusting wind blew more rain in through the opening.

"You didn't stick around long enough for us to thank you," I said, coming back toward the fire. "What's your name, mister? And what's with all this howling?"

The man lolled back on his saddle, stretching his legs out toward the fire. He acted more than a little drunk. His dark mustache and beard around his mouth were heavily salted with white. He looked to be about forty.

"My name? Huh! It hardly matters."

"We've gotta call you something."

"Well, if I gotta have a name, how about Kevin Michael Crozier? You can call me Chub."

"Chub?"

"For 'Chubby,' " he grinned. "A nickname."

"You're not exactly fat," Wiley said, backing up to the fire.

"Not anymore. That was years ago."

"Why were you singing and howling?" I persisted.

Crozier took another swig from the bottle. "I was singin' 'cause I was happy, and I was howlin' 'cause I thought you were Indians."

"So?"

"I just roll my eyes and start actin' strange and those superstitious redskins leave me alone. They think folks who are tetched in the head have the special protection of the Great Spirit, or some such drivel." He laughed again, and this triggered a short spell of coughing. He took a quick swig from the stoneware jug, then coughed and spat toward a corner. I detected a slight asthmatic wheeze in his breathing. The deathly white pallor I had noted on his face the first time we met was gone. What I could see of his face behind the tangle of hair and beard had a rosy hue to it, possibly the result of the liquor, his exertions, and the reflections of the crackling fire. He probably would have been a fairly nice-looking man without all that foliage and maybe a good bath and some decent clothes. Except for the addition of a stained canvas coat, he was dressed in the same clothes he had been wearing when I had first seen him. He suddenly fell silent, ignoring us as he stared into the flames, lost in a world of his own.

As Wiley and I tried to dry ourselves on either side of the hearth, the rain slashed down outside and the draft gusted in the window. Thunder boomed distantly, filling the silence. The pole and brush roof leaked dribbles of water in at least a dozen places, and the water sank in to the sand of the bare floor.

We still knew virtually nothing about this man who had been our benefactor, except his name, and I wasn't even sure it was his real one.

"What are you doing here?" I finally asked, hoping the man would open up.

He didn't reply for a few seconds, just continued to stare into the fire as if he hadn't even heard. Wiley took a stick and poked at the logs.

The pile of wood shifted, sending a shower of sparks up the chimney.

Finally he looked up at me, brushing a hand across his face, sweeping some of the hair out of his eyes. "I just don't know." Then he chuckled. "Sure I know; who am I kiddin'? But why should I tell you? I don't even know who you are." He looked owlish, as his eyes drooped with the liquor and the warmth. Gradually, his eyes closed and he sagged over against the saddle, breathing deeply in a drugged sleep.

"Shall we wake him?" Wiley asked after a few silent minutes.

Before I could reply, Crozier's eyes popped open and he looked blearily at me. "Where did you all come from on a night like this, anyway? How do I know you're not fixin' to rob me or kill me?" He dropped his head. "I guess you could kill me, but I sure as hell ain't got anything worth stealing."

"Where's your mule?" Wiley asked.

"He's tied up outside. I guess he's the only thing I have that's worth anything. But I'd appreciate it if you didn't take him; he's my only good friend, and I need him."

"Aw, shut up," Wiley said, exasperated, "and quit acting like a whipped dog. We're not here to rob you. We just want to know who the hell you are and where you're from and what you're doing out here. My name's Wiley Jenkins and this is Matt Tierney. We're out checkin' the mining prospects like 'most everyone else."

I was glad Wiley didn't identify me as a writer, so this strange man wouldn't clam up completely.

At this, his wariness seemed to dissolve. Even though he had told us his name and his strategy for staying safe from the Apaches, he had told us nothing about himself. And yet he had talked much more than he had the first time we met him. I attributed this to the more relaxed situation and the liquor.

"Hell, I'm forgettin' my manners. You boys like a drink?"

I shook my head, but Wiley said. "Sure," and reached for the proffered jug. He hefted it. "A might light, isn't it?" But he tipped the jug to his mouth.

"I wasn't expectin' company," Crozier answered. "But there's more where that came from, so drink up."

Wiley lowered the jug with a surprised look on his face. "That's some of the best brandy I've ever tasted," he declared. "And I've tasted some brandy in my time."

Chub Crozier's eyes crinkled in a grin. "I don't drink rotgut. As I said, there's more where that came from.

"Where's the photographer and that boy who got stabbed?" Crozier continued, changing the subject.

"The photographer is in his wagon, where we came from, about a quarter-mile from here. And the boy is still in the hospital at Fort Bowie."

"Fort Bowie?" Crozier perked up somewhat.

"Yeah. It was the only hospital close, and he needed more care than we could give him."

"Will he live?" Chub wanted to know, displaying more interest than I had yet seen.

"The post surgeon, Doc Donnelly, thinks so. Last word we got, he had developed an infection in the wound, but the doc thinks he can clean it up. He wanted to keep him there for another two weeks or so to make sure it was healing all right."

"Is he going to have any permanent injuries?"

"Not that we can tell," I replied, thinking that this stranger was displaying an unusual interest in the apprentice's welfare. "Doc thinks he may have a little numbness around that scar where some nerves are cut, but he should recover completely."

"Good." Chub Crozier stared into the fire once more.

"You out here prospectin'?" Wiley asked, throwing another small log on the fire that was beginning to die down slightly.

Crozier didn't reply immediately. "I'm out here living," he finally said without looking up.

"You may not be living long if you're just depending on that crazy act to fool the Apaches into leaving you alone," Wiley said, eyeing the shabby figure who was still seated on the sandy floor, arms over knees, facing the fire. Wiley reached for the stoneware jug again, tipped it up, and drained the last swallow from it.

"You've got a Southern dialect," Wiley observed. "But not deep south. Where you from?"

Chub Crozier shot a sharp glance at Wiley, but said nothing.

"I'm a Kentuckian, myself," Wiley said. "Don't worry. If you're running from something, your secret's safe with us. A man's past is his own business. Most men out here are making a fresh start from something back east."

Crozier still didn't reply, and I began to get the feeling that he was not so much eccentric as he was just plain crazy. Maybe the insane act he put on for the Indians wasn't really so much of an act. It could be that the Apaches sensed more about this man's mental condition than he sensed himself.

"Well, wherever you're from, or whatever you're doing here, you were a real godsend to us, and I want to thank you for it. If you hadn't snared us out of there, the best thing we could've hoped for was a quick death."

I motioned to Wiley. "Reckon one of us ought to go tell Burke where we are? He's liable to come looking for us."

"I'll go," Wiley volunteered, much to my relief. I had thrown off my poncho, but my damp clothes were not yet beginning to dry by the fire. At least I was warm.

Wiley put on his hat, picked up the Henry, and squeezed past the tilted door. The rain was still falling outside, but the wind seemed to have slackened up some. The thunder was less frequent and not as loud. The lightning still

148

flashed, but it was following the storm, which was apparently moving north, away from us.

After Wiley left, Michael Crozier bestirred himself, got to his feet with a grunt. "Going to check on Moses," he muttered, grabbing his hat off a hook on the wall.

"Moses?"

"My mule. Named him that because he led me to the Promised Land." With an ironic grin, he disappeared past the ruined door.

I started to take my rifle and follow him, but decided that he was too drunk to do me any harm. If he didn't come back, no harm done. He had left his saddle inside.

A couple of minutes later he was back, shaking water off his hat. Reaching under his coat, he pulled out another stoneware jug, identical to the one he had emptied earlier. It looked to be slightly bigger than a quart. The top of the bottle was a dark brown glaze, the bottom two thirds a tan color.

"Drink?" He held up the bottle. I nodded and reached for the jug. Uncorking it, I tipped it up and took a taste, rolling it around in my mouth before swallowing. Wiley was right. It was the smoothest, best-tasting brandy I'd ever put in my mouth. It even beat the most expensive that the *Silver Swan*, that fine Mississippi River packet, had to offer. I couldn't imagine where this man could have gotten such liquor, especially here. Maybe he and Shorty Anderson, the injured bartender at Dos Cabezas, had the same supplier who kept them in fine liquor. This Kevin Michael "Chub" Crozier, who looked like a prospector, smelled and dressed like a derelict, talked like a southerner, drank the finest brandy, and traveled alone in Apache country fascinated me more and more. My reporter's instincts were aroused, and I resolved to get his story, somehow.

For the time being, however, I respected his silence and hunkered down beside him, facing the fire and sharing the excellent brandy. The rain was tapering off outside, judging from the leaks in the roof and the sounds coming through the window opening. The lightning was fainter and less frequent. The thunder was grumbling and muttering in the distance. I felt sure the dry creeks and washes had not even crested yet. Probably not for several hours would the runoff from the mountains bring the desert arroyos to their high-water mark. It would be late the next day before our wagon could hope to cross the stream that had stopped us tonight.

The one-room stone cabin was apparently not even being used by Crozier as anything more than a one-night shelter. The only thing in the room besides the firewood was his saddle and canteen. The brandy had to be stashed outside somewhere — maybe on the mule.

I jumped for my rifle when I heard a slight noise at the door, but Crozier never moved or flinched at the sudden sound when Wiley and Burke came in. He either heard them coming early or was too drunk to pay attention.

Wiley had evidently briefed the photographer because Burke merely glanced around the room, nodded to me, and slipped out of his slicker. Burke sidled up to the fire, glancing at the still-silent Crozier.

Wiley packed a pipe from a pouch inside his shirt and lighted it from a blazing stick from the fire.

"Damn shame," Chub Crozier said aloud, staring into the flames. Nobody answered. "Shame about that boy, mister. Was he your son?"

"No," Burke replied. "He's my apprentice."

"Glad to know he'll be all right."

"Thanks."

"That bartender Shorty Anderson may not be so lucky."

I wondered how he knew about the bartender, but didn't interrupt. Maybe the brandy had finally loosened his tongue. He reached once more for the fresh jug.

"Always some damn ruckus," he continued, mumbling to himself and shaking his head. "Never let each other alone. Wouldn't be any trouble if everyone lived alone like me." A mirthless grin split his beard, and he tipped up the brandy again. If I had consumed only as much as I had seen him put away since we came in, I would have been out cold. Even so, the fatiguing day, the lack of sleep, the warm fire, and the few sips of brandy were combining to make my eyelids heavy.

"Always somebody buttin' into other folks' business. Like right now." He glared at us with watery eyes.

"Where is home?" Burke asked.

"Tennessee." He took a deep breath and let it out slowly.

"What happened?" Wiley asked quietly, trying to encourage his train of thought.

He snorted his reply. "Too many Yankees. Too much wife."

"What?"

He leaned back on his saddle. "I was young then — just out of the University of Nashville before the war. The city was a good place to live. A cultured place — you know, schools, libraries, good newspapers, lively politics. Business was good — steamboats landing and leaving by the dozen every week, farms prospering. There were horse races at Clover Bottom. Good saloons and restaurants. People went to concerts.

"I got a job as a clerk in the state legislature. Worked in the big new capitol building on the bluff overlooking town. It didn't pay much, but it was a good starting point for a young man with an education. Sure beat clerking in a store. I had no money and no head for business. And the nigger slaves did a lot of the manual labor. That is, they did it if you were wealthy enough to afford slaves. Most of the tradesmen and the city folks didn't.

"We saw the war coming, but even after it

started it looked as if Tennessee might not secede . . ."

I glanced over at Burke. We, or the brandy, had finally gotten this man talking, but it now looked as if we might be here all night listening to his life history.

". . . pretty stable," he continued. "I even got married while the war was in progress. Beautiful girl. Huh! If I'd a'had any foresight, I'd joined the army instead." He shook his head ruefully. "But the problem was I was torn in both directions, didn't really believe in slavery, but didn't want any outsiders coming in and forcing another way of life on us, either. It's always galled me to have somebody try to force something on me. But I kept my opinion to myself, took no part in politics, and tried to stay neutral as much as possible. Just did my job in the midst of all that hullabaloo about the secession. But my days of peace were about over. Ah, yes . . . Tennessee left the Union, and there were a lot of people on Capitol Hill asking why I wasn't fighting for my state and the South. I looked healthy enough to be in the army. As the war dragged on, the accusations got more and more pointed. I was called a coward, and worse, for not doing my share to defend the Confederacy. Yet there were quite a few others with abolitionist sentiments in the area. A lot of old friendships broke up. So I wasn't alone in my feelings. But each side thought of me as an outcast. They figured if I wasn't all for them, I was against them; there

153

weren't many neutrals."

"I know the situation," Wiley commented dryly. "I'm from Kentucky. But I was too young to enlist, and my father made sure I stayed out of it."

"Well, I finally got conscripted," Crozier continued. "Just in time to fight the Yankees who had marched up from Franklin. The war was lost by that time anyway, and they took Nashville about three months before Lee surrendered."

"What brought you out here?" Wiley cut in, trying to shorten this rambling story. "You an army deserter?"

"The occupied city and what came after the war made everything before seem like paradise," he said, ignoring Wiley's question. He put a hand to his face and rubbed his eyes hard as if trying to wipe away the memory of those past years. "Everything was disrupted, but the people left — mostly women and kids and invalids — still needed to live, so I didn't have any trouble finding a job after I mustered out. Got work as a laborer in a feed and grain warehouse. Also picked up a part-time job driving a delivery wagon. My wife and I got by, but those damn Yankee carpetbaggers came in there and just about took over. Got hold of some of the banks. Those fat, moneyed northern opportunists came in after the poor common soldiers had won the battles for them, and just bought up the choicest properties, farms, and elegant homes for the mortgages that were owed on them, or for practically nothing." His voice was sharply bitter. "Those years weren't as bad in Tennessee as they were in the states like Mississippi and Louisiana where they had a lot of illiterate freed slaves in the state governments ruled by Yankee generals in charge of those military districts."

"Reconstruction is over," Wiley interrupted. "Officially ended this year. All federal troops have been withdrawn."

"It doesn't matter now," Crozier muttered. "What more could they do to us? But it was bad enough then. My wife was a born Tennessean, but she saw how things were going and was all for supporting the winning side. Even though I had no strong feelings for the Confederacy, I resented the way those damn Yankees ran roughshod over us and our traditions and took advantage of the economic situation. Some of those men were ruthless. They destroyed a whole way of life that had existed for a hundred years or more. But, as I said, my wife began to nag me to take the loyalty oath to the Union — told me I'd never get ahead if I didn't. Me — a galvanized Yankee! Never! I was born and reared in the South. I didn't see any point to taking an oath that I wouldn't do what all the Confederate armies couldn't do — destroy the Union. It was the principle of the thing, ya know? Well, she commenced to rag me about it, and that woman never gave me a minute's peace day in and day out from then on. It wasn't just the oath. I was struggling to make a living. A lot of the freed niggers were taking the low-paying labor jobs. All the office jobs, especially in government, were given as political plums, so I didn't stand a chance there. I was clerking in this feed and grain store, as I said, with not much of a future in sight. We were barely making it, but I was so glad the war was over, I didn't really care just then. But my wife began to complain about the way we were living, especially as the kids began to come along. We had a boy and a girl within two years. It was tough, but the city began to rebuild and come back to normal, in spite of the Yankees. Well, my wife wanted a bigger house so we'd have more room. Even with my extra job driving a delivery wagon, we were still just barely getting by."

He paused in his narrative to lubricate his throat with a short pull at the brandy. "I couldn't do or say anything to please her," he went on. "I reckon she liked to gripe, or it just became a habit with her. Gave her something to do, I reckon. She just about wore my ears out. If it wasn't me, it was the kids or something that had gone wrong around home when I was gone. Yet she always worked it around somehow so that it was my fault, whether it was or not. You know what I mean?" He looked imploringly from one to the other of us. There was stony silence.

"Any of you-all married?" He shook his head sadly when we didn't answer. "Well, if you are, you know what I'm talking about. Got so I dreaded coming home to her, even after a ten- or

156

twelve-hour day at the store. I found a favorite saloon that had a pretty decent clientele of workmen and ex-soldiers, and took to spending more and more time there. 'Course that gave her more ammunition to blast me with and . . ." He glanced around at us more alertly and cleared his throat, raising his voice which had begun to sag lower and lower. "Didn't mean to bore you boys with this long tale. It's just that I haven't had a chance to really talk to anybody for a long time. But any married man would understand without me going into all the disgusting details. Things kind of went from bad to worse after that. She wasn't the charming, loving girl I had married a few years before." He shrugged. "I probably wasn't the same man, either. She accused me of drinking up my pay, and we got into some real rows." He leaned forward, holding his head in both hands. "God, how I used to dream of nothing so much as peace and quiet and solitude. Use to picture myself in a wood-paneled library in a house with the sun shining through the windows and the only sound the birds singing in the green trees just outside. And no bosses and no wife — no one to bother me . . ." His voice cracked slightly and he paused.

"To make a long story short, I finally just gave up and left. Got drunk one night after my boss fired me. He hired a freed nigger for less, who could sling more sacks of grain in a day than I could. I got home late, got screamed at. Walked out and headed for the river. Signed on as a

157

deckhand on a northbound packet with only ten dollars in my pocket. Had one helluva time working my way to the Ohio and then on to the Mississippi. I was big, but out of condition, and — well — you're not interested in all that. It's ancient history. That was six years ago. I finally made my way west. Figured nobody out here'd bother me, if I could keep the Indians off my back. But it seems it's getting a little crowded," he finished pointedly.

"You left your wife and two children?" Burke asked after a few seconds of silence.

"Huh!" Crozier grunted without looking up. "I'm not the heartless wretch you think I am. They're well taken care of — better than if I was there."

"How?"

"None o' your damn business," he snapped, showing the first signs of any temper. "And I've made provision for my wife and kids after I'm dead and gone."

"How so?"

"I've made a will, leaving the house and everything I own to her — under one condition. She must remarry after my death to get it. That way there will be at least one man in the world who will regret my death."

He doubled over with a deep laugh at his own joke, and the three of us looked wonderingly at each other. But his laughter turned into strangled coughing, and he again reached for the stoneware jug.

"Haven't you had enough of that stuff?" Wiley asked.

"The hell you say! Do I have to travel two thousand miles and six years to the Arizona Territory to listen to some stranger talk to me like my wife used to?" His voice had risen to almost a shout.

"Your cough sounds bad. That's all he meant," Burke said with unusual gentleness.

"Asthma," he managed to gasp. "One reason I came to the desert." His coughing and wheezing ended in a minute. "All the dampness and coal smoke in Cincinnati and Saint Louis just about did me in. This rain tonight is one reason I'm having so much trouble now."

I reached in and pulled out my watch. It was two-thirty. The storm had passed over: the many leaks in the ceiling were dripping only a little. After his long recitation, Crozier fell silent once more, and the rest of us sat staring into the low, flickering fire, entertaining our own thoughts. Even as I looked, a log burned through and shifted, sending a shower of sparks up the chimney. No one moved to throw another log on. I could hear the soft wheeze of his breathing as he slumped forward, leaning on his knees as he sat cross-legged on the floor.

This man was still an enigma to me. He had left several questions unanswered, even though he had given us a lot of his background — provided he had been telling the truth. How long had he been in this hostile country by himself?

He was apparently well-known to the soldiers of Fort Bowie, since the commanding officer had mentioned him to us the afternoon we'd spent in the CO's house. And the miners at Dos Cabezas knew him. Crozier appeared well fed, even though he was unkempt and very possibly an alcoholic. How could a penniless drifter afford the finest brandy? Maybe he had stolen a cache of it somewhere. And how was he providing for his family? Maybe he had faked his own death so they could collect his life insurance. But from what I knew of these so-called "insurance" companies, they would surely have demanded more proof of death before paying off. Even a dead body was not proof enough for some of them. Crozier spoke like an educated man, so maybe that part of his story was true, and Wiley had identified him by his dialect as a southerner, so maybe the rest of his story was also true. But there was still something about this man that didn't seem quite right.

"We'd better be getting back to the wagon," Burke finally said. "Hate to leave the stock unattended. In spite of this storm, the Apaches may be prowling. I've already lost one team to Indians. And I'd hate to think we had to haul that wagon by ourselves on foot."

I heard a snuffling sound. From where I sat with my back against the stone facing of the hearth, I could see part of Crozier's face as he leaned forward. He was crying. I attributed it to the maudlin stage of drunkenness.

"Good idea," I said, getting to my feet and stretching. "Let's go." I reached for my rifle and my poncho.

As the three of us headed for the door, Crozier didn't even look up.

"What'd you think of that?" I asked Burke when we got outside.

"Huh! A drunk feeling sorry for himself. Embarrassing to listen to."

"Well, he could have been a different person in his other life," I reminded him. "We didn't know him then."

He nodded his assent. "And he *did* save our lives."

Chapter 11

The morning dawned as one of those fresh, clear days that makes one glad to be alive just for the joy of seeing the country and breathing the air.

Shortly after it was light enough to see, we made a cold breakfast of crackers and cheese, since there was no wood dry enough to burn. Then we hitched up the mules, found our way back to the stage road, and started west once more. But not before we took a look at the stone cabin for Crozier. He was gone, leaving nothing but two empty brandy bottles and some warm ashes in the fireplace as evidence that anyone had been there the night before. Some mule droppings indicated where Moses had been tethered, and a few hoof marks that disappeared into the mesquite indicated he had circled the cabin and headed north toward the Dos Cabezas Mountains.

The rain had settled the irritating dust of the road — settled it into three or four inches of even more irritating mud. I was riding horseback again, feeling the sun climbing up the eastern sky behind me, warming and limbering my back as it might that of some night-chilled lizard on a rock wall.

Wiley and Burke rode in the wagon, and the

spare horse was tied on behind. The mules and horses slogged along, fetlock-deep in muck, except where the road became mostly sand. Then the footing was dry, almost as if no rain had fallen. All three of us were suffering from the effects of too little sleep, so were not inclined to talk, especially since we had not had our morning coffee.

Even before we came to the arroyo that had blocked our way the night before, I could hear the rushing torrent and knew there was no way we would ever get a wagon across. Burke drew up the mules a few yards short of it, and all of us stared silently at the surging, foaming mass of brown water that stretched more than fifty yards wide. Small trees and bushes swirled past us in the rushing current, and the grinding and tumbling of rocks and boulders mingled with the roar of the water to drown all other sounds, even our voices when we tried to talk. I could see by the debris that was scattered in a line a few feet from the water's edge that the level of the runoff was dropping. How quickly, I couldn't tell, but I guessed that no wagon or coaches would be crossing here this day.

I walked my horse close to the front of the ambulance, leaned over, and yelled, "Want to go back to Dos Cabezas and try it again in a day or two?"

The three of us looked at each other. Wiley and Burke shrugged and nodded. "Not much else we can do." Burke shouted back.

163

He backed up the mules a few steps and pulled them around in a tight circle. But less than a mile behind us, we encountered another gushing runoff that was too wide and deep to cross. We were cut off from retreat. So we worked our way back up through the desert shrubbery to our campsite of the night before. This time we kept going toward the mountains, hoping to reach a point where the water was shallower and we could cross and make a way back east along the base of the foothills to the camp of Dos Cabezas. But after almost three hours of blundering into blind passages, having to back out and turn or labor down and up steep, crumbling, sandy banks, and bouncing over rocks, the mules had to be rested.

We stopped where we were, and Burke set the brake and climbed down to have a smoke. "Damnedest thing I ever saw," he commented. "I've experienced some extremes of weather in this low desert country, but never too much water." He raked a match across a strip of iron on the wagon seat and applied it to his pipe bowl. "I think we'd be just as well off to stop right here and wait for this water to subside. T'hell with going back to Dos Cabezas. Doesn't look like we can get there anyway. We're cut off every way we turn and this is shaking hell out of my wagon and all the glass inside."

"Okay by me," I agreed.

"Come to think of it, this would be a good op-portunity to make some good views of this flood.

People back east who visualize the desert looking like the Sahara would never believe it."

"Good idea," Wiley agreed enthusiastically. "But we better get it pretty quick before the water starts receding. I saw a great spot about a half-mile back you could set up and shoot."

"Too bad these time exposures can't give a true picture of what this water really looks like," Burke said, climbing back into the driver's seat. "A time exposure I have to use will just smooth that raging flood into a silky, milky-looking stream. Won't really give a true idea of the force of that water."

He drove the wagon back to the spot Wiley indicated, and the three of us spent the next several hours, while the sun was high, rushing to carry gear, set up the tripod, carry the cases of glass plates, and move the wagon from one place to the other. Meanwhile, Paddy Burke prepared wet plates with collodian in the darkness of the wagon, brought them out and inserted them into the camera, and exposed plate after plate, rushing back inside after each two or three exposures to develop them while the solution was still wet.

By three-thirty he was finally satisfied. Dripping wet from the work in the humid, eighty-degree heat, we packed the gear away and leaned against the side of the wagon to rest. It was then that my grumbling stomach reminded me that we hadn't even paused for lunch. I was studying some of the glass-plate negatives Burke had placed on a box to dry in the sun. "How come the cloud formations don't show up in the sky here?"

Burke didn't even glance at the plates. "Collodian plates, being sensitive only to blue and ultraviolet light, cause blue skies to be over-exposed," he replied. "That overexposure eliminates the clouds. Too bad. Someday some smart photographer will figure out a way to capture those beautiful cloud formations. They'd sure add a lot to these spectacular views."

"These pictures will help build up my reputation and add to my repertoire," he continued, "but I still need something more unique, something that will make the public sit up and take notice of me. Something the other photographers can't duplicate. I don't know what it is yet, but I've got to have that special picture that will make my reputation. And I hope to do it with the stereoscopic view."

"Well, floods in the desert are rare and interesting, but I don't think you'll do it with pictures like you made today."

"How right you are. I could go over near Yuma where they're building the Southern Pacific Railroad east toward Tucson, but railroad pictures aren't a big seller anymore. Some lines even have their own photographers who take publicity pictures to use as advertising to lure tourists and settlers. The U.P. has a lot of land along its right-of-way, which it got free from the government and is trying to sell off to settlers that way." He chuckled dryly. "Some of those ads make Nebraska sound like Paradise."

"Maybe you should try for one of those railroad photographer's jobs," Wiley suggested. "Give you a steady income while you try for your one famous shot."

"Not for me," the Irishman almost shuddered. "Too restrictive. I like it out on my own, even if it is hazardous sometimes."

"Speaking of hazards, we haven't seen a sign of any Indians since your wagon was attacked near Fort Bowie," I put in.

"Not likely to, either," Burke replied. "But I'm not complaining. If we see 'em we're in trouble."

"Not really any place we can camp out here that will afford us much protection," Wiley said. "Want to spend the night in that cabin we were in last night? There's at least some dry wood still inside we can use for a fire."

"Not a very defensible place with only one man at a time to stand guard," I said. "One useless door, one window with no shutters, and a roof that's falling in and could be set afire with no trouble. They could be on us before we know it."

Burke shrugged. "The wagon's not too defensible either, as I found out earlier. I'd vote for the cabin. I think this floodwater is probably our best protection. That party that stole my mules and attacked me was probably just passing through. The men at Dos Cabezas didn't mention having much Indian trouble around here."

"Okay by me. It's the cabin, then," Wiley agreed.

By the time we gentled the wagon over some rough terrain to the cabin site, unhitched the mules and rubbed them down with an old gunny sack, and put on their nose bags with some of the oats we carried for them, it was five o'clock. While Burke was working inside the wagon and Wiley was gathering what dead wood and brush might be dry enough to burn to replenish the inside supply, I took my Winchester and walked a large circle around the cabin, always keeping within sight and sound of it. The structure stood in something of a clearing on a rise in the desert floor, as the land lifted toward the nearby Dos Cabezas range of mountains. Apparently at some time past, the mesquite, Joshua trees, ocotillo, and whatever else had grown there had been cleared away for a space of about twenty yards around. Then the fairly dense desert growth started again. I wondered who had constructed this cabin and why. Some prospector who had struck a promising claim nearby and wanted a more permanent shelter? The building seemed too small and too far off the stage road to have served as a stage station. It was about eighteen miles from the stone stage station in Apache Pass, which had been built for the old Butterfield Stage Line and still served as the station, so it was about the right distance for a change of horses. And maybe the original stage road had swung a little farther north at this point. Then again, the stone building might be much older than I realized, built by some Spaniard long before whites entered this territory. I would probably never know its true origin. Only one thing was certain — it wasn't the work of Apache hands.

I finished my circumspection and came back inside. Wiley had gotten a fire started, and Burke was bringing in some of our supplies and bedding. Before long, we had bacon sizzling and coffee boiling on the hearth. Fried corn cakes completed the meager menu. By the time the food was ready, we devoured it as if we hadn't eaten for days. I blistered my mouth on the hot bacon, I was so eager to get at it. It wasn't a varied meal, but there was plenty of it.

There's nothing like a full stomach to make a man see the world in a rosier light, and after supper we lighted our pipes and fell to discussing the mysterious Kevin Michael Crozier, who had entertained us in this cabin the night before. The horses and mules had been tethered with hobbles and a stout rope for a picket line just outside the open door by the wagon. We would also alternate guard duty. We would take all the precautions we could and hope for the best. Burke had warned us earlier that the Apaches habitually attacked only when the chances of success were great, when the enemy least expected it, and when their chances of loss were minimal. So it behooved us to be wary at all times. Too many whites, careless with overconfidence, were bleaching their bones in the desert sun.

"What do you think of this man Crozier?" Wiley asked us, using his shirttail to set the hot, blackened coffee pot off the fire onto the stone hearth.

"Crazy as a loon," Burke said shortly.

"I don't know," I said slowly. "There may be more to him than it appears. He may have all the wiles of a New York politician. Maybe he wants us to think he's crazy, the same way he fools the Apaches."

"He wasn't fooling with the amount of booze he was putting away," Burke said. "I thought only an Irishman who had never taken the pledge could drink like that. Besides, he didn't know we were anywhere around when you two heard him singing, so he wasn't acting then. Maybe he's just an alcoholic hermit."

"Could be the story he told us was true," Wiley put in. "I've seen a lot of southern boys done in by the war. Homes gone, family gone. The war, a nagging wife, economic pressures. Any one of those things could drive a man to drink."

Burke and I both nodded.

"He's a strange-acting one, all right. No doubt about that. No wonder the Indians leave him alone."

"But how does he live? Where does he get his food?" I asked. "How did he come by that mule and saddle? And that good brandy?"

"The mule and saddle he could have worked for. And Hawkins says he does odd jobs around the camps for handouts of food or tips. The brandy, I don't know." Wiley picked up one of the two empty bottles that lay nearby. "No markings or labels. But these glazed bottles look a lot like the bottles I've seen imported beer come in."

"Probably works a little here and there when he's sober, just long enough to get some money to buy food and liquor," Wiley concluded. "An asthmatic derelict who'll die alone in a cave or in the desert. The buzzards and wolves will finish anything that's left of him. He'll just turn up missing someday, and no one will ever know what became of him. His mule will be taken by the Indians or will revert to the wild."

We speculated a little further about Crozier, and when we ran out of guesses, the talk turned to other things. The coffee pot held just enough for one more cup each, and we relighted our pipes as the sun dropped over the mountains on the distant western horizon. Darkness came on quickly after a short twilight. There were none of the long, lingering sunsets this time of the year.

"Some of the boys at Dos Cabezas told me the camp at Greaterville is going strong. The miners there are still taking out a lot of gold from placers. Very little tunneling so far, and the camp is over two years old," Burke said.

"Where is it?" I asked.

"Just this side of the Santa Rita Mountains,

roughly seventy-five miles southwest of here. Then south of there, another thirty miles or so, is the Mowry Mine in the hills. It's been there for years and is still a steady producer of mostly silver and lead, with a little gold. Got a regular town there with a mill and the whole works."

"My job is to report on the newer strikes, but it wouldn't hurt to give an update of what's going on at Mowry."

"Will our supplies hold out 'til we get to Mowry?"

"That fella Hawkins at Dos Cabezas was telling me there's a well-stocked store and hotel called the Tres Alamos, on the San Pedro River just a little south of the stage station. Barring any accidents, we should reach there day after tomorrow," Burke said. "Hawkins says Tres Alamos is run by a man named Hooker and that his place has about anything a traveler could want, including decent meals at a decent price."

"Hell, civilization has moved right into the middle of Apache country." Wiley laughed.

"Well, if it has, it wasn't easy," Burke replied. "Hawkins said the first group of whites who tried to settle there about twenty-five years ago were all killed off by the Indians."

"Well, let's hope the place is safer now than it was then."

We drew straws for guard duty, and I came up with the last period, from about three until daylight. That would give me a least seven or eight hours of uninterrupted sleep. I was already nod-

172

ding over my coffee cup and was ready to turn in. We were taking all the precautions we could, and I felt relaxed and confident, looking forward to tomorrow. If I had known what was coming, I don't think I would have slept nearly as well that night as I did.

Chapter 12

The next morning we were on our way by sunup. The flash flood was gone as if it had never happened, even though there was still some standing water in low spots on the desert floor, which reminded me of portions of a grassy marsh. The stage road we followed west was washed out in several places and strewn with boulders, but our span of mules had no trouble hauling the ambulance up and down out of the dry, sandy washes. However, we had to stop twice and find some big sticks to break down the sharp, vertical banks that had been formed by the flood water. Even though Wiley was still somewhat sore from the cactus spines, he elected to ride horseback. We rode point on either side of the wagon, about a hundred yards ahead and fifty yards or so from the road, only coming back in to help when Burke was having a hard time negotiating a part of the washed-out road. We rode with our loaded rifles across the pommels of our saddles, our wary eyes sweeping back and forth, hoping to catch any unusual movement among the desert shrubs. For the first two hours I jumped at every rabbit, lizard, and roadrunner that darted across my horse's path. The sharp cactus of various species grew widely spaced enough to prevent our horses from cutting their legs, but we had to be very careful, nonetheless.

As the sun climbed overhead, the wrinkled gray-green flank of the Dos Cabezas slid slowly past us on the right. We didn't stop for lunch. The road curved slightly left in a long sweep around the last hill that could properly be called a mountain — part of the tail end of the Dos Cabezas.

As we passed, it wasn't the mountain that held my attention, but rather the playa — the normally dry lake that stretched out to our left, now a vast shimmering, flat sheet of water in the bright sun. Small desert shrubs that resembled clumps of buffalo grass were spaced so evenly on the desert floor that they appeared to have been planted. I made a mental note to ask Burke what they were called.

We made good time and reached the stage station called "Point of Mountain" at the northern end of this strange lake about two o'clock. Since we planned to push on as far as we could that night, we decided to stop for a rest and a meal.

There were three men living at this lonely adobe station — a big man in his mid-thirties who wore a week-old growth of coarse black whiskers and a permanent scowl, a young man about twenty who was tall and lean and blond and gave an impression of eager wonderment as if he were new to the territory. He functioned as a helper and did all of the unpleasant chores the older man didn't want to bother with. The third man was a young private in the U.S. Signal Corps who was stationed here as operator and repairman of the military telegraph that was located in a room adjoining the main stage station.

They saw us coming for a mile or so on the flat terrain, and were curious about us, as was natural for men stationed in such a lonely spot. But the older man didn't appear very eager to cook us up a meal at this time of day when there was no stage arriving. After seeing the color of our money, however, he fell to the job readily enough, while his younger assistant helped Wiley and Burke unhitch, unsaddle, and feed our stock. I was particularly happy to see the Army telegraph operator, since it meant I could get off my story. I got my leather dispatch case from my saddlebags, dug out a pencil, and hurriedly began writing at the rough, wooden table as the station tender prepared the food on the cookstove in an adjoining room. I had started writing up my notes the night before in front of the fire in the old stone cabin, but kept falling asleep, so had put them away for another time.

Shortly, the rough-looking station keeper brought in a feast of chili, beans, bacon, butterless bread, and the rankest coffee I had ever tasted. Wiley and Burke came in about the time it was put on the table. As we ate, I looked around the unadorned room, noting the four small loopholes in the corners of the thick walls. The corral holding the stage company teams was a six-foot adobe wall topped with broken glass. As I took another sip of the rank coffee, I realized one thing was missing.

"Where's the well?"

"There ain't one," the young man replied quickly. "Hafta haul all the water for us and the stock by wagon from some springs in the foothills several miles north of here. Damned hard job, too, for the pay I get . . ." He threw a glance at the older man, who ignored him. "No road, part of the way. The old wagon nearly shakes the kidneys outa me."

"Pretty dangerous, what with the Apaches and all," I said.

He shrugged. "If they get me, they get me. If they don't, they don't. Ain't much I can do by worrying about it. I carry a rifle, but I ain't so much as seen an Indian in the four months I been here."

"For that you'd best be grateful, young man," Burke said around a mouthful of bread. It occurred to me that it probably took the fatalism of youth to survive without cracking up in this part of the country. Then again, at the first sight of bloodshed, this youngster might very likely be gone, provided he wasn't the victim. The station keeper called the voluble young man to an errand outside, and Wiley and I helped ourselves to more of the hot chili.

While we were still eating, the young private came in. He was short and stocky, with a bristling mustache and the crossed flags of the

Signal Corps on his uniform sleeve. I introduced myself as a writer and indicated my desire to send a story over the government wire.

"Sorry, sir," he replied, "but I can't do that. This line has to be kept open for official army business and dispatches. The only civilian messages allowed to pass over this wire must be in the nature of an emergency. Is yours that sort?"

I had to admit it wasn't. And no amount of persuasion or offers of money to reimburse the U.S. Treasury for his services could dislodge him from his position. His devotion to duty and his orders was admirable but frustrating. I finally gave up, sopped up the last of my chili with a chunk of bread, and washed it down with the last of my coffee.

"How often does the stage run through here?" I asked, to change the subject.

"Twice a week each way," was the answer, "depending on the weather. We haven't had a stage from the east or west in several days — since before the rain started. The wire is still up, and I got the message from Tucson that the mail coach is held up there. Tucson had a lot of flooding. But that's not the problem. The San Pedro's flooded about thirty miles southwest of here. Coach can't ford it, and there's no bridge. The westbound stage left Mesilla over in New Mexico yesterday morning, so it's somewhere on the way." The young soldier helped himself to a tin cup of coffee and sat down at the board table. "If you want to leave your dispatches here, I'll see to it that they get on the first eastbound mail stage that comes through. Shouldn't be more'n a few days."

"Thanks, but I think I'll just hang on to them for now. I may have some more to go. And I need to do a little more work on composing my stories. These aren't just news dispatches."

"I'm just keepin' my fingers crossed that the line doesn't go down. I'm surprised some of those makeshift poles haven't washed out and popped that line somewhere. If it's not the Apaches, it's the weather. Every time it snaps I have to get a small repair crew from Fort Bowie or down from Camp Grant or Fort Apache. Repairing this damn line is the most dangerous part of this job."

"Have you had any run-ins with the Indians lately?" Burke asked.

"About two weeks ago they cut the line between here and Fort Bowie. While I was out trying to find it, I caught sight of a bunch of bronco Apaches. They didn't see me and I got out of sight — quick. They were headed south, drifting about ten head of horses. I found the cut where it went through a big mesquite. Got back safe that day, but in this country you never know."

We killed nearly two hours at the station, mainly to give our animals a rest. By four o'clock we were hitched and saddled and on our way again, heading south by west. The country here was open, its vast distances accentuated by occasional low mountain ranges that ran generally northwest to southeast. The vegetation was not quite as thick as it had been near Dos Cabezas, but the desert was still fairly evenly carpeted with sage, mesquite, creosote bush, prickly pear, ocotillo, and a hundred other species of plant adapted to this arid climate. However, it looked anything but arid now, with water standing in pools and marshy spots along the sandy stretches of the stage road. Wiley and I rode point as before, off the road and ahead of the wagon. The sun, having begun its downward slide, seemed to go rapidly, thrusting long shadows out across the flat land. The fiery ball dipped behind the distant low, brown row of mountains. The sky briefly lit up in a golden glow from the western horizon, and then the autumn darkness gathered quickly without benefit of a lingering twilight. We rode on, hoping whatever moon there might be would give enough light to see by. The road at this point would have been easy to follow, even by starlight.

Strangely enough, I felt a little easier in the dark, even though we were probably in just as much danger. Wiley and I pulled in to the road, still riding a good fifty yards ahead of the wagon. I felt lonelier in the darkness of this vast, open land than I ever had in wooded or mountainous terrain. An hour or so after full dark, the coyotes began to howl, sending chills up my spine and increasing the feeling of loneliness. Still we plodded on, our eyes and ears alert to any un-usual noises. Finally, sometime before midnight, some strange formations began to loom up in the darkness ahead of us, a bulk more felt than seen. As we got closer, I knew it was the huge jumble of rocks that had been our destination. The stage road wound directly through this strange geo-logic formation that looked as if some giant had dropped a gigantic wheelbarrow full of light-colored granite boulders and slabs. They ap-peared to have fallen in a huge pile that extended for a mile or two. It was totally unlike anything around it for miles. We wanted to get off the road and camp in the protection of the rocks, but it was difficult to find our way into this maze.

Burke pulled up the mules while Wiley and I scouted the base of the jumbled boulders for an opening. After about twenty frustrating minutes, we discovered one large enough and level enough to accommodate the wagon. The pas-sage led between two house-size boulders. About fifty yards in, the opening bent to the right and came to a dead end about thirty yards far-ther. At the elbow of this trail was the only place to turn a wagon and team around without un-hitching, but it would be a tight squeeze, never-theless. Some horse droppings and the soggy ashes of an old campfire indicated we were not the first ones to use this place. I had an uneasy feeling when I saw we were boxed in, but I kept the feeling to myself. We would be here only a few hours until daylight. We gathered enough dead brush from the desert floor outside to kindle a small fire for coffee.

While Wiley and I were engaged at this, Burke had swung the converted ambulance in a tight circle and parked it, unhitched and rubbed down the mules, and fed them some oats. Water was available for the animals and for us in the small pools of fresh rainwater trapped among the rocks. We made our campfire near the face of the almost-vertical granite slab that formed the abrupt end of the narrow trail. The wagon, mules, and horses were between us and the outside. Some narrow defiles formed notches at irregular intervals along the trail. Starlight and faint moonshine penetrated the narrow path, but our campfire threw the only real light. We were all tired and ready for sleep. None of us relished the idea of standing guard duty for what remained of the night. But we dared not get careless.

"Give me one more cup of that black coffee with a little honey in it, and I'll take the first watch," I volunteered. Wiley grinned at me across the campfire. For the first time in weeks, I noticed in the flickering light that his cheeks looked hollow, as if he had lost weight. His wavy brown hair had grown down over his ears and several days' worth of stubble furred his lean jaw. His eyes looked dull and tired. The indefatigable Burke hardly showed the wear and tear of little food, soakings in the rain, lugging heavy camera gear, driving his wagon all day, and sleeping very few hours at night on hard wood or ground. I was tired, but alert, and had volunteered for the first watch, to give Wiley some sleep. Daylight was less than five hours away. Without saying anything, I could take all of Wiley's watch and wake Burke about four.

There was really no rush; we could have slept in and laid over a day to rest up. There were no immediate deadlines or appointments we had to keep. But we felt safer camping away from any springs and resting only in the company and protection of camps, stage stations, or military posts. I had resolved even before coming to this territory that if I were destined to leave my bones bleaching in this desert, it wouldn't be for lack of caution.

Because of our fatigue, there was little conversation.

Shortly after we had scoured the tinware with damp sand and rinsed it out, Paddy and Wiley rolled into their blankets on the ground near the glowing remains of our campfire. Now that the rain was gone, they preferred to sleep in the open air on a ground canvas to avoid the chemical smell in the wagon.

Taking my Winchester, I ejected all of the cartridges and wiped the moisture from them on a dry cotton rag before reloading. Then I lighted my pipe and climbed onto the wagon seat to assume my lonely vigil. I opened the front and back doors of the ambulance, where it stood in the elbow of the trail so I could see my sleeping companions, in one direction, and the narrow defile leading toward the stage road in the other.

The horses and mules were picketed on a line that stretched from the wagon tongue to a scrubby mesquite bush that had somehow taken root in the crevice of a steeply sloping rock slab at the edge of the trail. The night was very quiet. If there was any breeze out on the desert, it didn't penetrate this sheltered spot among the giant rocks. The coals of the campfire were barely visible, winking through their layer of ashes. The slight movements of the animals on the picket line were the only sounds to be heard. My two companions slept without moving, their forms barely discernible lumps on the ground. After a short time, the absolute calm, the darkness, and the lack of someone to talk to began to make me drowsy. My head dropped, then I jerked myself awake, shaking the cobwebs from my brain. A minute later it happened again. I moved away from the corner of the driver's seat, where I had been resting my back against the upright body of the wagon, and forced myself to sit up straight. The effort to stay awake became torture.

Suddenly I jerked my head up out of an exhausted doze. Had I heard a noise? Wide awake and alert, I listened intently. Nothing. I was certain that what had awakened me was the noise of something hitting against rock. But how could I be sure? There was no excuse for falling asleep on watch. Many men had died because of just such a weakness. Had I imagined the noise, or somehow dreamed it in the few seconds I had dozed off? Maybe one of the horses had kicked a stone. Unless the sound came again, I would never know. On the other hand, someone could be out there, creeping up on our camp and I would never know it until the thrust of a knife, arrow, or lance put me beyond all caring. I was wide awake and nervous now. Maybe there was no reason for it, but I had to be sure. I stepped down quietly from the wagon seat and walked softly down the narrow trail between the boulders toward the stage road. I placed my soft, light boots carefully, making no sound, holding my Winchester, fully cocked, at waist level, and tried to pierce the darkness with my eyes. Every few yards I stopped and held my breath as I listened. I could detect no unusual sound. Proceeding thus, I came to the stage road and stepped out into it, looking carefully around, the half-moon shedding more light here in the open than in the shelter of the rocks. The desert night was absolutely still. Even the slight breeze had died.

Then I heard the soft whinny of a horse. I jerked around toward the sound. It was one of our horses. I slid quickly and silently into the shadows of the narrow trail between the boulders once more, still holding my rifle at full cock. Something had disturbed one of the animals. One of them snorted, and I could hear them shuffling around on the picket line. Could be a coyote or a skunk scavenging for the remains of our evening meal. Then again . . . As I got closer, I could make out the mules. They were out of position. The picket line had either been pulled loose or broken. As I slowed to approach them, something hit me like a sledgehammer from the side!

Chapter 13

I fell hard against solid rock at the edge of the trail, hearing my Winchester go off with a deafening roar as it hit the ground. Pain shot through my left shoulder, nearly numbing my left arm as I hit the granite boulder, but I instinctively twisted away from the weight of the figure attacking me. I caught the faint glint of a knife blade in the moonlight as I went down, and rolled toward my attacker, kicking his legs from under him while he was off balance. He grunted as he fell over me. I was on my feet in an instant and aimed a kick at the man's bulk in the darkness, not knowing what I would hit. My boot toe hit something solid, buttocks or leg, doing little damage. I didn't have another chance as he sprang to his feet and moved away from the wall between me and the stage road. I could barely make out his outline as he crouched. I didn't dare turn my back to look for my rifle on the ground near my feet for fear of instantly feeling the knife I was sure he still had. My left arm was nearly paralyzed with pain, and much to my regret, I had laid aside my heavy gunbelt when I went on guard, never imagining I would need my Colt or bowie knife.

The figure sprang and I leaped back out of

reach as the curving swipe missed my midsection.

"Hit the ground, Matt!" Burke's voice behind me yelled.

I dropped like a rock and a tongue of flame lashed over my head with the roar of Burke's Colt. He fired twice, one of the slugs whining off into the night. A voice cursed in fluid Spanish.

"*Bastante!* Don't shoot, amigo. I give up! *Madre de Dios!* My leg!"

"Hands over your head!" Burke commanded. "Stand in the middle of the trail where I can see you."

I felt around on the ground and finally located and retrieved my Winchester.

"Wiley, get some wood on that fire and stir up a light," Paddy continued as I got to my hands and knees and crawled back out of the way with my rifle. The horses and mules were milling nervously with the noise of the gunfire, but there was no place for them to go.

Suddenly, as if it had fallen from the sky, a blazing torch whooshed down from above us, almost landing on Burke's head. Paddy staggered back, colliding with me.

"No need for a torch," a voice said from the rocks above. "All of you stand where you are and drop your weapons!"

Wiley answered the command with a quick shot from near the wagon. An answering shot tore up the ground near his foot. Wiley dropped his long-barreled Colt and raised his hands. We were all illuminated and nearly blinded by the sudden light the big torch was giving off as it lay on the ground in front of us. I could finally see my attacker on the other side of the resinous torch. He was leaning weakly against the sloping rock, holding his right thigh where blood was staining the leather chaps decorated with silver conchos. He was hatless, and his mouth was a grim line. When he looked in our direction, the eyes were glittering beads of hate. The dark Mexican face looked vaguely familiar, but I couldn't really place it. Just now, however, my attention was distracted by the scuffling of boots in the broken rocks that formed the left side of the trail, and two men jumped down to face us, their guns leveled.

It was none other than Mad Dog and one of his men. He retrieved the torch, and the man with him — the short outlaw with the high-heeled boots and the tall, sugar-loaf hat — gathered up our weapons as Mad Dog motioned us back past our wagon. We obeyed numbly, without a word. I didn't know what my companions were thinking, but I was almost relieved that it was Mad Dog and not Apaches. I had an instinctive feeling that we would at least have a chance with these white outlaws that we would never have with the Apaches.

As we were herded back into the dead-end trail toward our fire, I tried to think what they might want with us, but my mind was not functioning very well at that moment. The feeling was slowly returning to my left arm, but my shoulder throbbed with a dull pain. I was aware of the short outlaw securing our horses and mules again on the picket line. Mad Dog waited patiently for the little man to finish with the animals and gather some brush to stoke up the embers of our campfire. No one spoke until we were all standing in a circle of blazing light. As I looked at the short outlaw again, I noted the bushy sideburns and the protruding ears and remembered him as one of the men with Mad Dog at Dos Cabezas. I wondered where the rest of his men were.

"You able to ride?" Mad Dog asked over his shoulder as the Mexican limped up behind him, still holding his bleeding thigh. His voice indicated he was ready to leave him if he couldn't.

"*Si,*" the outlaw hissed between clenched teeth. "Just *un momento* while I slice up that one for shooting me!" He glared hard at Burke, who coolly returned his stare.

"No time for that," Mad Dog said harshly. "Get that leg bound up and get the saddles and gear off our horses. We don't have much of a head start."

"*Aaiyyii,*" the Mexican whined. "You expect me to work in this condition? I am bleeding like a stuck hog!" As he spoke, he was unfastening his fancy chaps and taking his large, silk bandanna from his neck to tie tightly around his leg outside his trousers.

"You boys got some problem?" Burke asked,

with a mocking sneer in his voice.

"Shut up or I'll splatter you all over these rocks!" Mad Dog retorted, his voice almost shaking with rage. No one talked to Mad Dog like that and got away with it. I vividly remembered the incident at Dos Cabezas. This man wasn't known as Mad Dog for nothing. From the stories I had heard the miners tell, the sobriquet was well earned by his almost legendary outbursts of temper and irrational violence.

"You talk big with a gun in your hand." Paddy goaded him.

I wished silently that the redheaded photographer would keep still. This man was dangerous. The piglike blue eyes of the outlaw looked hard at Burke, but he didn't reply. Evidently these men were on the run and being closely pursued. The normally smooth-shaven face of Mad Dog was covered with at least two days' worth of stubble, and his eyes looked as if he had just come off a binge or he had not slept in many hours. They were after our horses and had tried to get them by stealth. A fresh change of horses might put them beyond the reach of any immediate pursuit. Burke knew what they were after, and I guessed he was talking back to them because he was furious at having his animals stolen a second time, even though the horses belonged to Wiley and me.

I glanced over at Burke and shook my head, frowning.

"You're damn lucky we're in a hurry, or I'd let Jacinto carve you up like a roast turkey," Mad Dog said, glancing over at the Mexican, who had finished tying the silk neckerchief tightly around his thigh and was sitting on the ground. "Keep your gun on them," he commanded his wounded companion. "Billy and I'll get saddled. You gonna make it?" he asked as an afterthought as he glanced at the drooping Mexican.

"*Si,* I'll make it," he retorted loudly, drawing his gun and leveling it on the three of us. "A lot you really care," he added in a lower voice as Mad Dog turned away toward the picket rope to help the short outlaw named Billy gather up our animals. In a few seconds I could hear them leading the two horses and two mules out toward the stage road, and in a couple of minutes they were out of earshot.

The silence settled in on the four of us. The fire, which had been blazing up with the addition of the creosote bush and small pieces of wood, began to die down, allowing the darkness to creep back in slowly. The flames still threw strange, dancing shadows on the granite boulders behind us. The three of us watched Jacinto, who was sitting on the ground, his wounded leg straight out in front of him. He was leaning on a rock with his gun arm resting across an outcrop. Our very silence seemed to make him nervous, plus the fact that we continued to stare at him. Maybe he sensed that, weakened as he was by the loss of blood and by shock, he might faint, al-

192

lowing us to jump him. With each passing minute, he grew more uneasy. He cocked his head to one side and listened intently. There was no sound. Any outside noise was effectively shut off by the huge pile of granite slabs around us. I got the feeling that he was in mortal terror that his partners in crime had deserted him.

Finally I heard the sound of thudding hooves, and the short outlaw with the tall sombrero appeared around the corner of the wagon, leading one of our mules that had been saddled and bridled. Jacinto glanced back with obvious relief. While Wiley, Burke, and I looked on helplessly, Billy helped Jacinto to his feet. The Mexican grimaced in pain as the blood-encrusted leg had obviously stiffened up a good deal. Still keeping a wary gun on us from a good twenty feet away, Jacinto allowed Billy to help him into the saddle. Just then Mad Dog appeared next to Billy.

"You're damned lucky I don't leave the three of you for the buzzards and coyotes," he said to us. "But I can't waste the ammunition, and I can't risk any more shots. There may be someone close enough to hear 'em." The close-set eyes in the round face looked hard at us for a second, and then he vanished into the darkness, followed closely by Billy on foot leading the mule as the mounted Jacinto clung to the saddlehorn with both hands.

"Damn! Damn! Damn!" Burke shouted in frustration as he kicked savagely at some loose stones on the ground.

"Did they take our guns with them?" Wiley asked, running for our wagon. He was back a minute later. "Can't find them. If they didn't take them, they must've thrown them up into the rocks somewhere. We'll never find 'em in the dark."

Then a thought struck me. "I left my gun belt and knife in my bedroll." I dug it out of the wagon and put it on and the three of us padded softly down the trail, out of the rock, to where it joined the stage road. It was silent and empty as if no one had ever been there. The half-moon had disappeared and the night was darker than ever with only the stars winking over the empty land. I shivered in the chill night air and was conscious again, as I moved my left arm, of the throbbing in my shoulder.

"Gone! Damn their hides!" Burke spat. "I hope to hell they run into some Apaches."

"You'd better hope we *don't*," Wiley said as we turned dejectedly back toward our camp. "We're afoot with only one pistol and one knife among us."

If either of them blamed me for letting down my guard and allowing this to happen, he never said it. I, for one, felt glad to be alive. With the release of tension, I felt a fatigue and weariness I hadn't felt in a long time.

"Might as well get some sleep," I suggested. Wiley and Paddy were agreeable. We gathered some more dead brush, threw it on the fire, and curled up close by. We were almost instantly asleep.

When I opened my eyes, sunlight was flooding our camp, reflecting off the pale slabs of granite around us. I rolled over and groaned involuntarily at the sudden pain in my stiffened left shoulder. I felt sure there was nothing broken, but it was sore as a boil. And, for the first time, I noticed the caked blood on the back of my right hand where a slight cut about three inches long angled back from between my thumb and forefinger.

Wiley and Burke were still asleep. I consulted my gold Waltham. It was 8:10. I was still tired but figured I could get by with the four or five hours of sleep I'd had. We had been lucky again; no Indians had come upon us as we slept without a guard.

By the time I had stirred up the fire set the coffee water to boil and the bacon to frying, the other two began to come awake.

Breakfast was a lively meal, as we discussed our next move.

"I'd estimate it's still a good day's march on foot from here to the next stage station on the San Pedro River," Burke said. "We'll have to leave everything here but our canteens."

"Don't think it'd be a might safer for us to lay over here today and rest up, and try it tonight?" Wiley suggested.

"Maybe so, but I'm anxious to get the hell outa here," Burke replied, ripping off a piece of dried biscuit with his teeth. I got the feeling that the headstrong Irishman was spoiling for a fight with the Apaches or anyone else who happened to cross him this morning. I was amazed that he had survived this long in hostile country.

"Before we do anything else, I suggest we scout the area for our guns, and maybe for any worn-out horses Mad Dog and his boys might have abandoned when they took ours," I said, trying to calm the agitated Burke.

He saw the sense of this proposal, so we spent the next hour after breakfast scouting the area around our camp, climbing among the jumbled rocks. Wiley finally stumbled upon our guns; they had been thrown by the retreating outlaws into the desert shrubbery about fifty yards from the turnoff to our camp. The Winchester, Burke's Henry and Colt, and Wiley's Colt were all empty, but I was greatly relieved to have them back; we had plenty of spare ammunition stored in the wagon. The right side of the receiver of my Winchester had a deep scratch running diagonally across the bluing, apparently where it had hit a rock. Then I took another look at the cut on my right hand and my ripped shirt-sleeve near the cuff, and a cold feeling came over me. It all matched up as I thought back on it. Jacinto had attacked me in almost total darkness. He must have lunged with his knife low, trying to disembowel me on the first thrust. Instead the knife point had hit the metal of my rifle and skidded off to rake the back of my hand and cut my sleeve as he slammed me into the rock wall. I smiled grimly. Jacinto, himself, probably would have said my guardian angel had been there to fend off the knife.

A few circling buzzards drew us a half-mile down the road to the carcass of a dead horse lying just off the edge of the rocks. He hadn't been dead more than a few hours, and the saddle galls and the dried lather on his flanks led us to conclude that he had been ridden to death by one of Mad Dog's boys. Any other mounts they might have had were nowhere to be found. They might have recovered and wandered off into the desert, or headed back from wherever they came.

We had recovered our guns but failed to recover any horses, so we finally came back to our camp about midmorning. After some discussion, Wiley's idea of resting through the day and proceeding on foot at night was finally agreed upon. We spent the day exploring the unusual rock formations in the immediate vicinity of our camp, and Paddy made several views of them with his largest camera and with the stereoscopic camera. This activity seemed to take his mind off the irritation of losing his mules.

We took turns standing watch and napping in the afternoon while the warm sun was high. Even Burke, who normally showed little fatigue, seemed to welcome the chance to rest. At least it didn't take him long to fall asleep. He didn't wake up for almost three hours.

In the late afternoon we fixed up a hearty

supper of bacon and beans, and we baked up some biscuits to eat and carry with us.

After supper we rummaged through the wagon, selecting and rigging up what little we planned to carry.

"Don't get too ambitious, boys," Burke cautioned. "We've got a good twenty-five-mile hike ahead of us, and no telling what we may run into on the way. Be best to travel light."

The one thing we didn't skimp on was our ammunition. We filled our cartridge belts and divided up another two hundred rounds among us, making sure we had the right shells for our various weapons.

The next most important thing we carried was water, each of us filling a two-quart canteen. There was probably still plenty of standing rainwater along the way, but we were taking no chances. Besides that, all we had was our jackets, hats, boots, and some extra biscuits and bacon.

The sun slid down over the horizon, and the sky directly over our rock fortress turned a deep blue in the brief twilight.

Burke took a last look inside his wagon, then climbed down and shut the back door. "Sure hate to leave all my cameras and gear out here unprotected. Any saddle tramp could come along and make off with the whole wagon, or haul off my expensive cameras and sell them. Then, again, the Indians might find the wagon and burn it just for spite."

"Of course," Wiley said with a straight face,

"the Apaches could get us out there and then we wouldn't have to worry about the wagon."

Burke grinned, but I'm sure the thought of Apaches was on his mind as much as it was on mine and Wiley's, as we shouldered our light, makeshift packs and set off in the gathering darkness.

Chapter 14

The night march proved to be long and tiring, but uneventful. The stage road was washed out in places, but the walking was fairly level, and my light, supple boots were made as much for walking as for riding. Another thing I was grateful for was the light cloud cover that obscured the moon.

We struck no lights, even to smoke our pipes during rest stops, and we kept our talking to a minimum. It was a quiet night, with even the normally vocal coyotes holding their peace. A light breeze was blowing almost into our faces from the northwest, and the air had a slight smell of more rain.

Even with our fairly slow progress, we found ourselves nearing the San Pedro stage station. It was about 3:00 A.M. by my watch. We halted where the road curved close to the riverbank. We could barely make out the squat, adobe buildings that comprised the stage station less than a half-mile away on this side of the river. We debated whether or not to go any closer in the dark for fear of being shot by some nervous station keeper or guard. We finally decided to stretch out where we were and rest until daylight. Even if we weren't shot at by mistake, we reasoned, there was "no good reason to rouse those folks out of their bunks at this time o' the night," as Wiley put it.

We made ourselves as comfortable as we could down behind some clumps of sage, out of the cool, predawn breeze, and dozed off, secure in the belief that we were hidden from any casual passersby.

Just before the sun thrust its head over the eastern Dragoon Mountains, we strode into the stage station, announcing our arrival with plenty of noise and shouts. Smoke was coming from the stovepipe chimney on the flat roof, so I knew someone was up and about.

While we were still some ways off, a man appeared in the open doorway, rifle in hand. As we got closer we had our hands in the air, loudly proclaiming our good intentions.

The man in the doorway was tall, lean, and of indeterminate age, with a drooping handlebar mustache and a prominent Adam's apple. His black hair was combed straight back and fell nearly to his collar. The black eyes on either side of the hooked nose regarded us steadily with no hint of a smile.

"Where'd you boys come from and where are your horses?" were the first words out of his mouth when we got close enough to hear.

We explained briefly what had happened to us before he lowered his rifle and invited us inside.

"The missus is just fixing us some breakfast. You're welcome to some. Don't reckon y'all have et much on the road."

After our hike and my nap, I could've eaten the bark off a corral pole if they hadn't already been peeled, I assured him. Not only that, but we had money to reimburse him for any grub we might consume.

"No need for that," he waved aside our offer to pay. "You're welcome to such as we've got. Fact is, I'm glad to see a few more gun hands. You can use those guns you're packin', can't ya?"

We assured him we could hold our own. "What's the problem?" Burke asked. "Indian trouble?"

"Hell, no! I guess Mad Dog didn't tell you what they was runnin' from, then?"

We shook our heads as we shoveled in mouthfuls of flapjacks soaked in maple syrup that his wife served up on tin plates. She was a quiet, sandy-haired woman who, in a softer environment, would have been stout. But her short figure and arms appeared to have solidified into muscle with the work this remote station must have required of her. Her hair was drawn back in a bun, and wisps of gray mingled with the ash-blond. Time and the sun had etched some fine crow's feet at the outer corners of her eyes, yet the bone structure of her face and her blue eyes hinted at a Nordic ancestry and considerable beauty in her youth.

". . . thought we was hot on their trail," the station keeper was saying as my attention was abruptly jerked back to the conversation, "or

Mad Dog woulda sure left you for buzzard bait."

"That's about what he said," Burke replied. "Didn't want any more shots fired, even though we'd already done some shooting."

"By the way, the name's Jonathon Saunders." He stuck out his hand and each of us introduced ourselves in turn. "This here's my wife, Ingrid. We run this place as best we can by ourselves. At least we did 'til yesterday. That's what I was fixin' t'tell ya. Mad Dog and his boys come ridin' in here late in the afternoon and threw down on us with no warnin' atall. There was four men up from Tres Alamos — a hotel and store about three mile downriver — waitin' for the stage. Had almost two hundred ounces of gold dust and nuggets in my safe that was due to be shipped on the first westbound stage for Tucson. The miners from Greaterville had been depositin' it with me for the past week or two. Well, we figure Mad Dog knew that we had at least *some* gold, since there hadn't been no stages through here in either direction in a week due to the floodin'. River's higher'n I ever seen it — muddy, swift, and treacherous, with no good fords anywhere. And no bridge."

He paused in his narrative to pour himself a cup of coffee from the big pot on the cookstove. For the first time, I noticed how bloodshot his eyes were. He didn't appear to have had much sleep.

"Well, sir," he continued, "they come bustin' in here — rode up from south o' here as well as anybody can recollect — got the drop on us and threatened to shoot everybody on sight if I didn't open the safe. I didn't have no choice so I done it. Whilst they was loadin' the bags o' gold into their saddlebags and forcin' my missus to get 'em somethin' to eat on the trail, one of the men who was waitin' on the stage saw a chance to draw his derringer and fight 'em. And sure enough, he drilled one of 'em behind the ear. Well, Mad Dog flew into a rage, and he and his men started shootin'. They was slugs flyin' everywhere in here. We all hit the floor and the one who had drawn first was killed. But Mad Dog wasn't satisfied with that. Nosir. He takes and cuts the dead man's privates off, and his Mexican friend slices up the body like some o' the Apaches hereabouts been known to do. Then they shot another man in both knees and both elbows, and threw both the dead man who was mutilated, and the live one who was crippled, into the river. I guess that musta satisfied 'em, 'cause they rode off east up the stage road. They didn't even bother to bury or carry off their own man who'd been the first killed. Reckon they was scared off 'cause some boys come ridin' up just then from Tres Alamos." He paused and wiped a sleeve across his eyes. "Two good family men dead for no reason. Helluva price to pay for not much more'n five thousand dollars' worth of gold. They'd a done better robbin' a bank — and currency's a lot lighter to carry than gold."

I held up my coffee cup to accept a refill from

Ingrid Saunders as her husband continued his story. "We were in shock at first; then we moved to see if Jason Fetters had survived. He was the man they shot in both knees and both elbows. You can see for yourself that river's up and roiling. High, muddy, and swift, with lots of quicksand. We never found him, and it come on to dark, and me and the boys was so damn mad we got up a posse and took off after Mad Dog and his men. They'd gone straight up the stage road. Well, they had nearly an hour's head start on us, what with lookin' for Jason and all that. We didn't see hide nor hair of anybody. 'Course they could've turned off anywhere. By the time we got to the Texas Canyon rocks, some o' the boys begun to cool off and think about what a good place for an ambush that would be. There was only five of us, and our horses were pretty well blown by then. We got to arguin'. A couple of them wanted to go on, but about three wanted to turn back. Goin' up against Mad Dog in the dark was more than they bargained for. So we come on back. Got back just before daylight. Had to walk the horses most of the way to save 'em. That was yesterday morning."

"Good thing you decided to turn back," I said. "They *were* hiding out in those rocks and could've cut you down from ambush."

I popped the last forkful of food into my mouth and sat back with a contented sigh. "Too bad we didn't see which way they went when they left with our horses and mules."

"Don't matter much," Saunders replied dejectedly. "There ain't no telegraph here anyway, so we can't wire ahead to Fort Bowie or Fort Apache. Like as not they're headed for Mexico."

"I don't know. They may have to get help for that Mexican, Jacinto. He had a bullet in his leg. He wasn't in very good shape the last time I saw him," Burke said.

"What happened to the body of the outlaw who was killed?" Wiley wanted to know.

"When we got back yesterday mornin', he was lyin' out, stiff, in the storeroom. Me and two o' the boys in the posse took him in the wagon down about four miles from here and buried him in the desert. Even slapped together a pine box out of an old packing crate. Pretty decent, considerin' what they did to our two — just threw 'em in the river, and one of 'em still alive, yet."

"Where are those other men who were in the posse?"

"They went on back to Tres Alamos to wait a couple more days to see if the river drops so the stage can get across. No sense in 'em hanging around here. No place for 'em to sleep. They didn't think me and the missus would be in any more danger from outlaws. And we haven't seen no Injuns around here for at least a month."

"Mad Dog's gettin' quite a reputation in the territory," Burke remarked. "I've been hearing about him and his gang terrorizing this part of the country for months."

"He sure is," Saunders nodded. "Military can't seem to stop him. If we don't get some law in this territory soon, some o' these outlaws — Mex *and* American — are gonna figure they have a free hand in Arizona. They're gettin' to be worse than the Apaches."

"As you can see, we're in bad need of some horses," Burke said, changing the subject. "You got any you can sell us?"

"None that I can spare," he replied thoughtfully. "The stock that doesn't belong to the stage line I have need of myself. You might try down at the Tres Alamos. C. H. Hooker runs the place. He's been there two or three year, and he keeps a few extra horses. He'd probably sell you some. Don't know what kinda mounts they'd make. Some of 'em is half-broke mustangs, and maybe a few army rejects, but it beats walkin'."

We thanked him, paid for our breakfast over his objections, and set out to hike the three miles downriver to the hotel/saloon/fortress called Tres Alamos, declining the station keeper's kind offer of a ride in his wagon.

"It's a little community, a few miles downriver." He gestured over his shoulder. "Some tough folks with a few cattle on land near the hotel — Bill Gibson, Wally Roberts, and some others. The stage station used to be there. Even had a telegraph and a school for the kids. But the Americans, and later the Mexicans, got run off, or killed off, in the past ten years."

We found Tres Alamos looking pretty much like Saunders had described it. Standing about four hundred yards from the San Pedro River and partially shaded by two big, heavy cottonwoods, was a two-story hotel built mostly of adobe and reinforced with cottonwood beams, wooden porches, and window frames. The walls were a good two feet thick and the windows narrow. The front door, swung on cast-iron hinges, was made of three-inch-thick oak planks. From the outside it had the appearance of a very solidly built fortress, but the whitewashed interior was comfortably furnished with bright, woven Indian rugs and two chandeliers, made of wagon wheels, hanging from the ceiling in the main lobby that doubled as a saloon and card room. Javelina heads and antique rifles decorated the walls. The kitchen and dining room were adjacent to the lobby, and the upper floor was given over to a dozen rooms for guests. The place was nearly full of men waiting for the waters to recede so normal stage operations could resume, but the three of us were lucky enough to secure the last room available. Apparently, the proprietor, one C. H. Hooker, was doing a great business, and not just in his hostelry. Behind the main lobby and saloon, running the full width of the building, was what amounted to a general store crammed with all kinds of goods, including liquor, cigars, groceries, blankets, lanterns, boots, nails, and a long list of other items. And the best thing about it was that his prices were reasonable, as we discovered. Meals were fifty cents, beds, seventy-five, and everything else was priced proportionately. He did, indeed, have horses which he rented for a dollar a day. When we asked him about buying some, he hesitated only a minute before quoting us a price that was more than fair for two geldings and a mare we picked out. The mare and one of the geldings were Morgans, probably no more than four years old, which looked strong enough to pull Burke's wagon with no trouble, provided we lightened it up a little. We would have preferred mules, but Hooker had none that he could spare at the moment. We rented saddles and bridles for the day until we could recover our own gear, which we had left behind with Burke's wagon.

It was after 9:00 A.M. by the time all this was concluded, and we were anxious to get started back for Burke's wagon so we could return by nightfall. We rented three more horses as spares so we wouldn't have to ride the Morgans that would be pulling the wagon back, and to have some spare mounts in case of Indian attack.

Some of the men killing time in the saloon asked if we'd like them to ride along with us for protection. They were getting bored, anyway, they indicated, and were looking for something to do. I was leery about riding with total strangers, but Burke and Wiley were agreeable, so three more men joined us. They introduced themselves as Walter Logan, Jim Barrett, and

Cyrus McGillicuddy, miners from Greaterville, a few miles to the south, who were waiting for the stage to Tucson. McGillicuddy, at about thirty, was the oldest of the trio, while the other two were constantly joshing and playing practical jokes on each other. After talking to them a few minutes, my wariness relaxed. I had become, over the years, a fairly shrewd judge of men, and had acquired some sixth sense that could detect, within a very short acquaintance, if a man was to be feared or trusted. And according to that instinct, these three could be trusted. Even so, I let it slip in the conversation that we were just three working men who had nothing much to steal, just in case my hunch proved wrong.

The weather had faired up, the night clouds had blown away, and our ride to the Texas Canyon rocks, as Saunders had called our camping place, was uneventful and pleasant. If any Apaches had us under surveillance, they never showed themselves. A well-armed, six-man party with three lead-horses held no allure for them. We found the wagon and our gear undisturbed where we had left it, and had shortly hitched up the two Morgans, tied the other horses on the back, and were on our way back. The Morgans were not accustomed to the harness, but Burke managed them very well. While on the way, we regaled the three miners with the full story of our encounter with Mad Dog's gang, both in Dos Cabezas and in the rocks. It turned

210

out that McGillicuddy was one of the men who had been at the San Pedro stage station when Mad Dog's bunch robbed it and killed the two men. And Logan and Barrett had helped bury the outlaw who had been killed.

"A very dangerous man," Cyrus said, referring to Mad Dog. "Besides being mean, I think he's got something loose up here." He pointed at his head. "But he's the worst of several bandits in this area. We've had several Mexican bandits hit Greaterville in the past year who are crueler than the Apaches. Luckily, I was gone to California when they hit last year. Tortured and killed three men in the camp, besides taking their money and guns."

We arrived back at Tres Alamos about eight that night, after stopping at the stage station to check on Jonathon and Ingrid Saunders. We had missed supper, but the cook, who was used to fixing meals at all hours, obliged us by heating up some roast beef and beans. Afterward we ambled into the bar in the next room and joined our three friends and a few other men in a drink. Two of the tables had card players. I smoked my pipe and drank two beers before weariness overtook me.

"Gents, I'm going to turn in. I can hardly keep my eyes open," I finally said, when I could no longer keep my mind on the conversation. I later regretted that I hadn't pushed myself to stay awake, because by going to bed at ten-thirty, I missed one of the strangest epi-

211

sodes I'd ever heard of.

It seems that after I left, Burke, Wiley, McGillicuddy, Barrett, and Logan got into a poker game. Wiley treated to a bottle of the best whiskey the bartender had. While they played and drank, their tongues got looser, and they began discussing the gun battle at the stage station. The longer they went, the louder they got, and some of the other men in the bar joined in the conversation as Cyrus McGillicuddy related the details of the shooting. Sometime in the early hours of the morning, Logan raised his glass in a toast to the two men who had been shot and thrown into the river by Mad Dog.

"Here's to 'em, even if their bodies are never found. They have a fitting resting place at the bottom of the San Pedro, whose water gives life to this land!"

Everyone cheered and there were more toasts and a few maudlin tears shed for the dear departed, even though many of the men in the room hadn't even known them. Then someone remembered the outlaw who had been killed by the derringer and buried the next day in the desert.

"Did you know him, Cy?" someone asked.

"Never saw him before. Young man, in his early twenties. Fairly nice-looking gent. Probably trying to make a name for himself and a lot of quick cash by hooking up with Mad Dog. He must have thought he was safe, since Mad Dog's got everybody in this territory buffaloed."

Then, as Wiley related it to me, someone asked McGillicuddy to repeat again the details of what started the fray. He told them the four outlaws rode up to the station, came in, and ordered drinks from Mrs. Saunders. Just as she was pouring them, Mad Dog drew and ordered her husband to open the safe. That's when Mike Johnson, the man with the derringer, drew and fired, killing the young outlaw.

"Did that outlaw who got drilled ever get his drink?" a man interrupted before Cyrus could finish repeating this story for the third time.

"No. As I recollect, the drinks were still settin' on the bar when they finally rode off," Cyrus replied. "I remember thinkin' how odd it was that not a drop had been spilled in the fracas."

"That's a damn shame," the man remarked. "That fella gave his life for ridin' with Mad Dog and didn't even get one last drink before he checked out."

"Here's to him, whoever he was and wherever he is!" shouted another, tossing off a jigger of whiskey.

"I say we go dig him up and give him one last drink to wet his whistle in hell!" yelled the first man.

There was a drunken chorus of approvals at this suggestion, Wiley later told me. "And I was one of them. It seemed like the appropriate thing to do at the time," he explained. "Well, the idea just took hold," Wiley continued, as he and I sat alone at a late breakfast the next morning in the dining room. Burke was outside in his wagon darkroom making some prints from some glass negatives.

"The bartender tried to put a damper on the whole business when he saw we were serious," Wiley said, pouring himself some more black coffee. "But he didn't stand a chance with that bunch. Several of us grabbed bottles of whiskey and headed for the door, with Barrett, Logan, and McGillicuddy to show us the way where the outlaw was buried. One of the miners did remember to grab a pick and a couple of shovels from his gear for us to use. Several of the boys were so drunk they could hardly sit a horse, so they hitched up a team to a buckboard instead. By this time it was about an hour or so before daylight, and black as pitch outside, except for the stars. We blundered around in the desert and rode about five miles before Barrett finally found the spot where the unmarked grave was. 'Course, by that time we were all thirsty again, so we had to sit around and have a few more snorts. By the time it began to get daylight, somebody suggested we ought to start digging. So we unlimbered the shovels and started digging out the loose dirt. We hit the top of the pine box only a foot or two below the surface. We pried the lid off, and by then the sun was just beginning to poke its head up over the horizon. There he lay in that box with his eyes closed and his hands crossed over his stomach as peaceful as if he'd just stretched out for a nap." He paused to wipe his plate with the last of his flapjacks and fork the bite into his mouth. Except for a tired look around his eyes, he showed surprisingly little sign of his wild night.

"Well, we lifted him up outa that box and he was still stiff as a poker. Then . . ." He was interrupted as Paddy Burke came through the door, holding several dripping prints by their corners. "Did they come out?" Wiley asked, as Burke kicked a chair back and sat down.

"Clear as crystal," the redhead replied triumphantly, spreading the wet paper out on the tablecloth for us to see. I shoved my plate aside and pulled two of the six prints toward me.

"Lucky I remembered my stereoscopic camera, and luckier still that the sun was coming up and I had enough light. "I had to hurry and prepare some collodian plates. But caught up with the boys by the time they blundered around out in the desert, looking for the spot."

As Burke talked, I was looking at some amazing photographs. There was a shot of the dead man lying in the pine box in the shallow hole, with several men standing at the head of the grave. Then there were three different views of the dead man on his feet, being supported on each side by mustachioed miners. The dead man was tall and wearing boots, dark pants, a jacket, and a collarless shirt. His eyes were closed, but he appeared to be grinning, his lips drawn back

215

in a fixed grimace of death. One of the side views showed the bloodstains behind the ear where the derringer slug had struck him, but it had apparently passed through the base of his skull without disfiguring him. The next two views showed one of the miners pouring whiskey from a bottle between the dead man's clenched teeth, while the body was being held up by Wiley and McGillicuddy.

"After we'd given him his last drink, put him back in his box, and covered him up, some of the boys got mighty quiet," Wiley said. "Reckon maybe they were sobering up some and thinking about how they might wind up someday."

"Anybody recognize him?"

"No. He must not have been from these parts, or one of those men would surely have seen him before. He had no identification on him. McGillicuddy said he checked his pockets before they buried him."

"Damn! These are pretty gruesome," I remarked, looking again at the pictures. "Who would believe this if they didn't see it with their own eyes?"

"Nobody would," Burke replied, picking up two of the prints and waving them to dry the paper. "That's why I've got these. I'll need to reverse the twin images I had of each of these views and get them mounted on my cards. If you think these are something, wait 'til you see them in a three-dimensional stereopticon."

"They're pretty weird, all right, but do you

think this was the big shot that will make your reputation?"

"Maybe not, but it'll put me well on the way."

Chapter 15

In spite of getting no sleep the night before, Paddy spent all day printing and mounting his views of the dead man's last drink, and still found time to make several formal portraits of some of the flood-bound men at Tres Alamos. Many of them also bought stereoscopic card views of the previous night's episode as souvenirs. And all of his customers paid in gold — coins or dust.

We all got a good night's sleep and struck out the next morning for Greaterville, the rich gold camp about forty miles southwest as the crow flies. In order to get there, we were faced first with the problem of crossing the flooding San Pedro. The extra day we spent at the hotel helped some, because about fifteen miles downstream from Tres Alamos, we found a spot where the river was spread out in a wider bed, and the water level appeared to be down about two feet from its previous high level.

Wiley rode his horse into the stream, testing the bottom. The muddy current was swift, but the water was only about three feet deep, and the footing proved to be solid all the way across. So, muttering a prayer under his breath, Burke eased the team and wagon down the bank into the water, then slapped the reins across the backs of our Morgans, yelling encouragement as they lunged into their collars. The team managed to keep up the momentum long enough to get us to the far bank, some forty yards away. We paused there to let the horses blow while Burke checked to be sure nothing inside was wet. A few wooden cases had been dampened, along with a couple of barrels, but the water had not soaked through.

We made our way back north to hit the stage road and then turned west for about twenty miles. Shortly after turning south at the Cienega stage station, we made camp for the night.

The next morning we continued following a faint, two-wheel road through the dry country. After several miles it began to rise and dip, bending gently along the western edge of the low Santa Rita Mountains. We crossed and recrossed a small stream about six times. It was hardly deep enough for the horses to wet their feet in most places. I suspected that in the summer months the watercourse was probably dry. The land had a silent, empty stillness about it that gave me a lonesome feeling. The gentle south wind rustled the dry bunch grass along the road, and occasionally a big hawk or buzzard could be seen soaring noiselessly far overhead on the thermals. The vast desert country, gray-green and tan, stretched out in all directions, humped up and wrinkled here and there into low mountain ranges. It was a land that had the look of changeless eternity. I was riding horseback while Wiley and Paddy rode the wagon. As we slowly moved down this long, winding road, we might have been the last human beings on earth. Who would have known that it was, even now, being savagely fought over by white men and red men? In spite of my reverie, this very knowledge kept me alert, my loaded Winchester across the pommel of my light, McClellan saddle. I had chosen to ride the one available horse almost by default. Burke and Wiley Jenkins were not that keen about spending hours at a time in the saddle, preferring the somewhat more comfortable seat of the sprung converted ambulance. But I delighted in the sense of freedom that being astride a tall horse gave me. Even though the two muscular Morgans pulling the wagon were also good saddle horses, I had dipped deeper into my poke to buy the Arabian I rode. The bay gelding had caught my eye, and Hooker had at first declined to sell him, arguing that he kept him as a rental horse for special customers only. But I finally made him an offer that he couldn't afford to pass up. And I got the feeling that this horse, whom I named Samson for his strength, could lope all day and never tire. Even though slightly smaller than the Morgans, he carried my 165 pounds, my light saddle, saddlebags, and bedroll as if he had nothing at all on his back.

The farther we went into the Santa Rita foothills, the more we began to notice something yellowish covering the hills and valleys. On closer inspection, we discovered that the yellow cover was actually millions of small, bright yellow flowers. Whether it was the warm October days or plentiful rain that brought them out, we didn't know. Nor could any of us identify with certainty the type of flower it was.

"Looks like the Lord has showered the whole area with fine gold dust," Wiley remarked.

"In more ways than one," Burke replied, clucking to the team as they reached a slightly steeper grade.

At about noon the road forked, as we had been told by the miners that it would. The main road, going straight south, led eventually to Mowry in the Huachuca Mountains near the Mexican border. We followed the branch that turned off to the right, toward the flank of a bulky, treeless mountain about five miles away, where Greaterville was supposed to be located.

A little over an hour later we arrived at this two-year-old gold camp. It was comprised mostly of a few dozen small adobe and rock cabins, several semipermanent tents with foundations, and roughly two hundred men, along with an assortment of mules, wagons, rockers, shovels, and other gear. Nearly all supplies were brought in from Tucson or Tres Alamos.

We were greeted with mild interest, until the miners had gotten all the news of the outside that we could provide. When they found we carried no mail, they went back to work. By some judicious questioning we found out that this camp,

221

unlike many others, was still obtaining plenty of gold by placering, without the need for sinking shafts or tunnels to follow the veins or deposits. Water for washing the gravel had been a problem for months, until the recent rains had made every dry creek bed a running stream, so the rockers and sluice boxes could be used. The men who were mining away from a running stream had to pack their rock and gravel and sand into canvas sacks to carry to water over a mile away, to wash out the gold — or pack the water in canvas sacks to take where the ore was.

We heard stories that during their first two years of operation, the men working Greater Creek, Smith's Creek, Sucker Run, Boston Gulch, and Mac's Creek here on the southeast side of the mountains had taken out in excess of $100,000 in gold. We were told that some fifteen months previously a Mr. Candelario had found a nugget weighing more than twelve ounces and that a year ago last month, a man named Joe Herring had taken $162 out of his claim in a single pan of dirt — one chunk alone being worth $150.

Another thing we noticed in the few days we remained at Greaterville was that this camp was not rowdy, and no fights occurred. Everyone went about his business and got along unusually well with his neighbors. Few disputes arose. And unlike Dos Cabezas, this camp was well-organized to protect itself against any and all intrusions from the outside. Even though we were probably no safer from Apaches here than any-where else, I felt a much greater sense of tran-quillity and slept much sounder than I had at any time except for our stay at Tres Alamos or Fort Bowie. I got the distinct feeling that Mad Dog would not fare well in this camp. He probably knew as much, since in spite of its gold, we were told, he had never attempted to rob it.

During our short stay at Greaterville, Burke did his usual good business among the miners, making formal and informal portraits of them. They were cash customers who paid in gold nug-gets or placer dust. Burke also dragged out his big, seventy-pound field camera and made a few views, for his own use, of the camp and the placer workings on the slopes.

The weather remained fair, with warm days and cool nights. Our initial interest in staking a claim was cooled when we found that every known source of placer gold on this side of the mountain had been staked and recorded. This didn't prevent us from poking around on our own, which we did, with no success. With persis-tence, time, and luck, we might have been able to rake up and sift out a little dust that had been overlooked by the hordes of men who had been crawling over this mountain for two years, but we decided against staying, for several reasons. Burke indicated he wanted to go back to Fort Bowie and pick up his apprentice. He was also eager to replace the Morgans with a team of four good mules as soon as possible. We assumed that the water had receded sufficiently for the stages to resume running.

As we prepared to leave, a young man whom we had seen prospecting came up to us and introduced himself as Wilbur Joisteen, a recently discharged army sergeant.

"You boys going on south?" he asked.

"No. We're headed back toward Fort Bowie," Burke told him.

"Oh." The ex-soldier looked disappointed. "I was hoping you were headed for the Huachuca Mountains. I wanted to travel along with you for protection."

"Where you headed?" Wiley asked.

"Mowry. I'm not having much luck here."

"They've been taking silver and lead out of the Mowry mines for about twenty years. Probably not much left there for a newcomer, unless you want to work for wages."

"Not me. Had enough of that during two army hitches. I want to strike off on my own," the young man said. He was a short, sandy-haired man with a stocky build, who carried himself with a relaxed air of confidence.

"Things have kind of fallen apart down there," Joisteen continued. "There have been several owners in the past few years. Don't know if the mines are playing out or what. But," he added with a grin, "if there was that much silver at the Mowry mines, there's bound to be more in other locations nearby in those mountains. Who knows? There may still be some pickings at

Mowry, or thereabouts."

"How far is it from here?"

"Oh, maybe another thirty miles. It's only a short ways north of the border."

"You know, I wouldn't mind having a look at Mowry, myself," I said. "It would work in well with my articles for *Harper's Weekly*. Sort of a comparison between the old, established mining community and these new camps."

"I guess it wouldn't hurt to take a look, as long as we're this close," Burke said. "My apprentice can wait a few more days."

"I've got my own horse and gear. I won't be any trouble. Just want to ride along. The boys here tell me there's not nearly as much traffic back and forth down that way as there was even last year."

"Why's that?"

"The decline in production of the Mowry mines, and the Apaches," came the prompt answer.

"If that's decided, then, let's go," Wiley said.

Rather than saddle up, I trailed my Arabian on behind the wagon and rode on the seat with Burke. Wiley and the ex-sergeant rode horseback on either side of the wagon.

The road south to the Huachuca Mountains was well defined. The recent rains may have settled the dust for a time, but numerous heavy ore wagons and strings of pack mules had churned it quickly into a deep, loose powder once more. The hooves of our team and the other horses, along with the wheels of our wagon, quickly churned up the inches-deep dust in the still air. The morning was warm — almost sultry — with a high, thin haze of clouds. We stopped only briefly around noon to rest the animals and stretch our legs, walking away from the road to breathe some fresh air and drink from our canteens.

In the early afternoon, the road swung abruptly to the left, leaving the gently rolling country to enter the steeper, wooded hills. The few open hillsides were covered with thousands of the long-stemmed, yellow wild flowers we had seen earlier near Greaterville. The deeply rutted road climbed gradually into the hills that were covered with oak, juniper, and manzanita. The dust boiled up around us in a choking cloud, sticking to our moist skins, coating our faces, lips, and throats. We quit talking because of it. Burke and I could hardly see Wiley and Joisteen riding only a few feet away. The only relief came when we crossed and recrossed a small, rocky stream every few hundred yards and paused to let our animals wet their muzzles in its clear water. As the fine clouds of powdery gray whirled up around us, we tried to breathe shallowly. Burke squinted his eyes until they were barely slits in his face, and let the horses have their head. We could barely see, but there was no way the team could wander off the road without our being instantly aware of it, due to the narrowness of the small valley we were passing through.

I pulled out a black silk neckerchief I had bought at Tres Alamos, wet it from a canteen, and tied it around my mouth and nose.

A burst of gunfire exploded from the woods a few yards to our right. Joisteen's horse squealed and fell hard against the side of the wagon. Burke pulled back on the plunging team while I had my Colt out and was firing through the dust pall at some dim figures in the woods. Bullets were thudding into the wood beside me. Wiley's horse was down and kicking in the road ahead of our team, blocking them from running. More shots exploded and I could just make out some brown bodies moving among the trees about twenty yards away. Apaches!

I emptied my pistol. As I got up on one knee and turned to reach into the wagon for my carbine, the team reared backward. The sudden jerk of the wagon caught me off balance, and I tumbled off the seat over the wheel.

"Down! Hit the ground!" I heard Joisteen yell. I was already there, rolling aside to keep from being stepped on by the wildly leaping team.

"Here they come. They're making a rush!"

Then the brown, bare bodies were among us and it was every man for himself. I had no idea where Wiley, Burke, and Joisteen were and no time to think about it as an Indian appeared about three feet in front of me. Except for a red headband and a breechclout, he was naked, his muscular torso gleaming with oil. I sprang to my feet, reaching in my belt for the only weapon I had left — my bowie knife. He lunged at me, his knife aiming for my chest. Desperately I reached up to block the blow and managed to catch his right wrist with my left hand and stop the blow above my head. I swung my own knife toward his midsection, but he caught my wrist in a viselike grip. For a few long seconds we stood, straining, glaring at each other, locked onto each other's wrists. He was taller and heavier than I, and I could feel my grip slipping from his oily skin.

With a quick motion, I stepped forward and tripped him. As he fell back, he pulled me with him, twisting as we hit the ground. Before I could get away, he was on my chest. His left hand still held my right wrist, and his right knee pinned my left arm. I struggled against his superior weight, but it was no use. I was helpless, while his knife hand was free. With a wild cry of exultation and triumph he leaned back.

The next few seconds seemed frozen in eternity. I could see the glint in his black eyes as he hesitated slightly, savoring his moment of victory and the look of panic on my face. I knew my time had come and quickly willed my soul to God. But panic was followed by a flash of anger. Was I going to let some greasy savage stick me like I was a frightened deer? The knife came plunging down and I twisted my head to the right. The point missed my throat but pinned the silk neckerchief to the ground as the blade sank deep into the soft earth. For a second, as he tried to pull the knife free, his hand was within reach of my teeth. I snapped his thumb and bit down hard. He howled in pain and jerked back, but I bit down even harder, knowing my life depended on not letting go. He let go of my wrist and reached across with his left hand to pull his knife free of the ground. My knife hand was freed for a second. I plunged my blade into his side under his left arm once, twice, simultaneously giving a convulsive lunge to throw off his weight. I was wild. Three more thrusts between the ribs of the sagging body and my assailant was gasping his last in the dust of the road.

I looked around. The dust was still billowing up, but not as thick as before. The Apaches were retreating! Two of them were dragging one of their wounded companions. Two other Indians lay sprawled at the side of the road. I backed up against the wagon and looked quickly back and forth. Joisteen lay facedown a few feet away, near his horse, both apparently dead. Two more shots exploded from the other side of the wagon and Burke appeared with his Henry. The hammer fell with a click, and he lowered the barrel, since the Indians were already disappearing up the hill into the oaks and piñons.

"Where's Wiley?" I yelled.

"Come back here, you red savages! I'm not done with you!" Burke shouted at the retreating Indians, his face beet-red.

"Where's Wiley?" I asked again, coming around the wagon.

Wiley Jenkins came staggering up the slope

from the other side of the road, one hand to his head and his nose dripping blood.

"You shot?"

He shook his head. "No. I just got hit in the head with a rifle butt."

"You okay?"

He nodded. "I will be in a few minutes."

We quickly compared notes. Burke was unhurt. Wiley had a lump on the side of his head and possibly a broken nose. Joisteen was dead, cut down by a bullet through the throat. His horse was dead and so was Wiley's. One of the Morgans had a slight wound near the top of a neck muscle. I was unhurt, but as my breathing steadied down and I realized the immediate danger was past, my knees began to feel weak and it was all I could do to climb back into the wagon. I retrieved the Apache knife that was still pinning my neckerchief to the ground near the body of my attacker. I put the knife and the handkerchief away in my bedroll as a memento to be looked at later and pondered over. It might help me fasten onto the reality of what had just happened. I was almost in shock from the suddenness of the attack and already it hardly seemed real, as the dust settled and the woods grew quiet.

But I dared not relax yet. Burke was gathering up the loose reins and telling us to get into the wagon. My Arabian was still tied on the rear and was not injured, although he was rolling his eyes and dancing around, trying to jerk his tether loose. We put Joisteen's body in the back and climbed to the seat. Burke skillfully backed the spooked team and turned them around in a space so tight I would never have thought it possible.

"I don't know about you," Burke said, as he maneuvered the rig, "but I've suddenly lost interest in Mowry or any other thing these mountains have to offer."

"Poor Joisteen has too," Wiley said.

I nodded numbly, scanning the shadowed hillsides as I fingered cartridges out of my belt loops to reload my Colt.

"Can't figure out an attack like that," Wiley said as Burke urged the horses to a trot, and the wagon went through a ford in a shower of spray.

"Trying to terrorize the whites, or trying for our horses maybe," I said. "Or our guns."

"They dragged off their wounded, but there were several bodies left behind."

"Guess they thought they could surprise us in that cloud of dust and cut us all down without much danger to themselves."

"What were they — Chiricahua? Mescalero? Tonto?"

"Don't know and don't care," Burke said, his mouth grim. "But the murderin' savages got more than they bargained for."

When we again reached the rolling, treeless foothills, Burke pulled the team to a stop while I saddled my horse and rode alongside, my Winchester held ready. We took our time and continued traveling back toward Greaterville as night came on. We did not pause for food or anything except watering the horses at a stream ford where Wiley washed the blood from his nose and face.

We finally reached Greaterville shortly after midnight. The miners met us and took charge of Joisteen's body while we poured out our tale of the attack.

"Damned dangerous down that way lately," one of the men remarked. "Those Apaches will hit when you least expect them. Have to be on your guard all the time. I don't go much beyond the confines of this camp by myself. When we go up to Tucson or Tres Alamos, we always travel in groups of at least ten — well armed."

We doctored the wounded Morgan as well as we could, by sterilizing the bullet hole. The slug had passed through the muscle of his neck, about an inch from the top, near the base of the mane. Our team was very tired, so he offered little resistance when we cleaned the crusted, dusty wound and swabbed it with alcohol. Then we rubbed down the horses and fed them the last of the grain we carried, before settling down for the night ourselves.

As I unrolled my bedroll on a spot of soft sand beneath the wagon, the Apache dagger and my silk neckerchief fell out. I picked up the knife. Instead of the artistically crafted weapon I half expected, I found only an ugly, foot-long piece of steel resembling an "Arkansas toothpick." It was

fashioned from the business end of an army bayonet. The handle was wrapped in rawhide and
the edges of the tapered blade were honed to a
razor sharpness. The man it had belonged to was
past caring about it now. I wondered if his companions had come back for his body, or if it was
still lying in the dusty road. His blood was still
staining the sheath of my bowie knife. But it
could very easily have been the other way
around. The warrior who attacked me was unusually large for a race whose males were mostly
short and wiry, built more for endurance than
for sheer strength.

My pulse quickened as I recalled the details of
that struggle. Life had never seemed more precious to me than it did in those few seconds
when I was about to lose it. Even now, several
hours later, I was so keyed up, I couldn't calm
down enough to sleep. The stars in the black
vault of the heavens twinkled beautifully. The
smell of the night air, the sound of the wind
softly rustling in the dry grass — all common-
place things — were objects to be noticed and sa-
vored — and appreciated. I marveled at things I
had barely noticed twenty-four hours before.
This heightened sensitivity was a direct result of
my near-death. This will to live was a strange,
powerful force. Logically, the struggle to survive
as long as possible seemed foolish. Death, that
great leveler, would claim us all, friend and foe
alike, within a few short years, anyway. But this
thought never crossed my mind when I was

pinned to the ground and saw that dagger coming toward my throat. It was pure instinct that saved me.

I took a deep breath and let it out slowly as I stretched out on my blankets, conforming my body to the soft sand beneath me.

The next morning we made sure that the miners knew how to contact Joisteen's family before we pulled out. One long, slow, and careful day of travel put us back at Tres Alamos. Logan, Barret, and McGillicuddy had gone on their way and the hotel was no longer crowded.

After supper we discovered a lean, hard-eyed man with a drooping mustache, who had arrived from Tucson the day before. His name was Tobias Cameron and he identified himself as a United States marshal with a federal warrant for the arrest of Mad Dog. In addition, the warrant included Jacinto Cruz, Billy Fannin, John Carlson, and Justin Asbury. The first two names were the only ones familiar to me, unless Billy Fannin was also the "Billy" of the short stature, the tall sombrero, and the jug-handle ears who had attacked us at Texas Canyon rocks.

"There are others reported to be riding with this Mad Dog, but these are the only names I have," Cameron told the seven of us who were gathered in the saloon of Tres Alamos. He had treated to a round of drinks, but that was not necessary to get our attention. The crowd that had been at the hotel on our previous stop had thinned out due to the resumption of stage service.

"I was appointed by Territorial Governor John Hoyt to go after this gang. They're giving this territory a bad name. The Apaches are another matter. That problem is in the hands of the military. But the governor is very sensitive about the image of the territory. The eastern press has picked up on this Mad Dog and made him sound like the slickest border bandit who's ever outwitted the law, instead of a half-crazy bully who guns down unarmed victims. In short, the newspapers and dime novels have made this outlaw known throughout the country, and the territorial government is embarrassed about him. They don't see him as helping the territory's chances toward statehood, either."

"Statehood?" one of the men asked. "What statehood?"

"The politicians are already thinking ahead. Governor Hoyt is young, but he's got big plans for Arizona. He figures it's not too early to start cleaning up the territory's image." He shrugged. "So that's why I'm here. No pictures exist of this man or his gang that we know of, except a few drawings on some wanted posters. So I'm looking for volunteers for a posse — preferably men who've seen him and know the way he operates. And it wouldn't hurt if you don't mind some hard riding on short rations, and can handle a gun to boot."

Three of the men who were listening came forward to get more details.

"Remember, boys," the marshal cautioned them as Wiley, Burke, and I moved away to stand near the bar, "this man's more than just another outlaw. He's like a test case to show the rest of the country just how territorial justice works. If we catch up to them, they're not to be gunned down unless there is no alternative. They are to be brought in for trial. The governor was very clear about that. So if any of you don't want to sign up on those terms, now's the time to say so. You all know the danger involved. I have the authority to deputize as many men as I need."

"How long do you reckon this'll take?" one of the men asked. "My partner's working my claim, and I can't be gone more'n a couple of weeks."

The marshal shrugged. "Who can say? Depends on where he is. We have no authority to go into Mexico after him. He's on the run, but I imagine he feels pretty secure, since there's virtually no law in this part of the territory. And he can always retreat into Mexico if things get too hot. He'll probably find out soon that I've been sent down here after him, so the sooner we get started, the better. I'd like to surprise him if I can."

"What's the pay for this-here job?" a grizzled older man asked.

"The undying gratitude of your government," the marshal replied with a straight face.

There was startled silence for a second, and

then the group broke into a guffaw.

The marshal grinned and struck a match to his cigar. "Actually," he said, blowing a cloud of smoke at the ceiling, "the territorial government is offering a ten-thousand-dollar reward to the man or men who bring this Mad Dog in for trial."

There was a low whistle and general nodding of heads at this.

"I'm not eligible for the reward myself," the marshal continued, "so the reward would be split among the men riding with me — *provided* we capture him and don't kill him. If he is killed, each man would get only his daily pay."

"Which is?"

"Two dollars a day, and you supply your own horses and guns."

"That ain't much, considerin' what's involved," one of the men muttered.

"That's double a cowhand's wages," the marshal countered.

"We ain't cowhands. We're miners. I could take in more from my claim at Greaterville than that. And not get shot at into the bargain."

The marshal shrugged again, squinting at him through the cigar smoke. "Like I said, this is strictly a voluntary assignment. I don't want any men who aren't committed. And there's a chance at a share of that reward money. I reckon you have to be part gambler if you took to prospecting and mining. There's as good a chance of this gamble paying off, I suspect, as there was when you went looking for gold."

" 'Scuse us, Marshal, while we discuss this," one of the men said, drawing his two companions away to the other side of the room.

I turned back to the bar and signaled the bartender for another beer. "What do you think of volunteering?" I asked Burke and Wiley.

"Not much," the New Yorker replied. "I'm a photographer, not a manhunter. I'm not one to back off from a fight, mind you," he hastened to assure me, "but I'm not going looking for trouble for two dollars a day."

Wiley was silent for a moment and then said, "I think I'll let it pass, too. That reward money is tempting, but there are just too many unknowns. I don't like to ride with men I don't know. They may panic if they come up against Mad Dog unexpectedly. From what I've seen of Mad Dog, he's not about to be where you expect him, and I'll wager he's not about to be taken alive, either."

"Well, whoever goes after him, I hope they get him," I said. "Maybe put the fear of God into some of those other border bandits."

"Don't count on it," Wiley replied. "Easy money is a mighty strong temptation, especially when the chances of getting caught are slim."

The marshal was rising and shaking hands with each of the three men he had been talking to. "Be saddled and ready to ride at first light," he told them as they moved away. "I'll swear you in in the morning."

"Marshal," I said, as the three of us approached him, "if you haven't already heard the story, we can give you some of the details of our latest run-in with Mad Dog."

He motioned for us to sit down. "You wanting to join the posse?"

We declined the invitation, but gave him a brief account of the episode at Dos Cabezas and about being robbed of our stock in the Texas Canyon rocks later. We finished off with what we had heard about the robbery and shootings at the San Pedro stage station.

When we finished, he nodded. "C. H. Hooker, who runs this place, was telling me about that stage station affair. Sorry I got here too late to talk to an eyewitness."

We mentioned the drunken party when the dead outlaw had been given a drink.

"What did this dead outlaw look like?" he wanted to know. Burke and Wiley described his appearance, and Burke even went out to the wagon and brought back some of the prints for him to look at. Cameron studied them carefully, holding them closer to the light of the coal-oil chandelier. "Did he have brown hair?"

We nodded.

"That just about fits the description I have of John Carlson, one of the men named on my warrant. Now, describe Mad Dog to me."

We obliged, giving him a detailed image of the man. He nodded thoughtfully. "That's a little different from the way I pictured him. I'm much obliged to you boys. Can I buy you another drink?"

We declined. "In that case," he said, tossing his dead cigar butt into a brass cuspidor, "I'm going to turn in. Tomorrow's going to be a long day."

Chapter 16

"I reckon the Apaches probably done us a favor, even if they wasn't meanin' to." Jonathon Saunders chuckled at the irony of it as he poured himself a cup of coffee and sat down at the table with us. It was an hour after sunrise the next morning, and the three of us had stopped at the San Pedro stage station to check on Saunders and his wife before we started for Fort Bowie. One other purpose of our visit was to ask again if he had any mules for sale.

"Are you sure it was one of Mad Dog's men?" Wiley asked.

"Well, the boys who told me about it had just rode in from down south near the border where they'd been doin' a little prospectin'. They was the ones who buried him. The body was muti- lated — arms and legs sliced open, stuck full of arrows — and looked like he'd been burned in a fire before he died. But the description of his face matched the description of a Justin Asbury — mole on his eyebrow and all — that Marshal Cameron read to me off his warrant early this morning."

"If that's right, then that's two of the gang the posse won't have to worry about," Burke said. "Unless they've picked up some more recruits along the way."

"I don't know about that," Saunders said, "but when Marshal Cameron heard about it, he and his three-man posse hit south outa here like the devil himself was after 'em."

"Between the Apaches and the posse, maybe we'll be rid of Mad Dog and his gang," Burke said. He set his coffee cup down and wiped his mouth with the back of his hand. "Now, about those mules . . ."

Saunders had bought a strong pair of mules from two prospectors who had gotten discouraged, sold out, and taken the stage east three days earlier. Burke made him a good price for the animals and we harnessed them up. In order to lighten the wagon as much as possible, Wiley rigged a pack saddle for each of the two Morgans who had been relieved of their pulling chore, and we trailed them on, single file, behind the wagon when we pulled out an hour later. One of the pack horses held the stereoscopic camera, tripod, collodian plates, dark tent, a few ounces each of iodide of potassium and cadmium, bromide of ammonium, hard rubber bath for solutions, hydrometers, nitrate of silver, plate holders, and several other items to make up a self-contained, portable photographic outfit.

"It's what I used to carry into the mountains and places where I couldn't take the wagon," Burke explained. "It's compact and it gets the job done, even though I'd prefer to have all the room and things the wagon offers. Besides, I

242

almost missed those pictures of the dead outlaw the boys gave a drink to. I don't want to be caught unprepared again. In this occupation you don't often get a second chance."

"Say, what do you make of that business that Saunders was telling us about?" I asked as I kept my Arabian, Samson, at a walk alongside the wagon.

"What business?"

"About those two pokes of gold somebody left for the families of the two men murdered by Mad Dog at the stage station."

"I don't know," Wiley replied. "Seems strange. Could be the other miners from Greaterville just took up a collection and didn't want anyone to know who had done it."

"I guess that could be. Saunders said he found it outside his door a couple of days ago with a note as to whom it was for. He put it on the next westbound stage for San Diego to deliver it to their families. Estimated those pokes contained about a thousand dollars each."

"Seems a little odd that his friends would want to remain anonymous, though," Burke mused. He was silent for a few seconds. "You don't suppose there's any connection between that and the gold that was left at Fort Bowie for Shorty Anderson, the injured bartender, do you?"

We looked at each other blankly. "Could be. But who?"

We had no answer, and our speculations soon wore themselves out.

We reached the Texas Canyon rocks about two o'clock and stopped for a short time to rest the animals and have a smoke. Then we pushed on toward the Point of Mountain stage station, arriving there about suppertime without incident. About five miles out from this station, Burke pulled the wagon over to let a westbound stagecoach pass, the first one we had seen since we were last at Dos Cabezas before the floods.

Over the plentiful supper of stew, we quizzed the army telegraph operator about the latest happenings. I didn't realize how starved for news I had become since we were out of touch with the rest of the world. Nothing of note had come over the wire, he told us, except routine army business. The Apaches had been fairly quiet, although in the past few days reports had come through from Fort Huachuca that a few scattered bands had been raiding the isolated ranches and mining camps farther south, along the Mexican border. We could attest to the accuracy of that report. The rest of the bands who had bolted the reservations earlier were either holed up in the Sierra Madres in Mexico or in the Dragoon Mountains that heaved their bulky vastness against the southeastern skyline, uncomfortably close to where we sat. The army brass, although they would not admit it, were embarrassed by the free comings and goings of this so-called Mad Dog, who had been terrorizing the territory. They had paid little attention, the corporal told us, until the territorial governor had gotten involved and offered a reward for his capture. I remembered that Major McCullough had told us it was the responsibility of the troops to protect travelers and other whites not only from the depredations of the Indians, but also from *any* outlaws. At least that was so in theory. Practice was quite another matter. Even if the military posts had been up to strength, patrolling so vast a land effectively was a virtual impossibility. Therefore, outlaws both red and white roamed pretty much at will, with little concern for the blue-clad troopers who daily ventured out on patrols from their strategic outposts.

Realizing this, the governor had ordered a special lawman into the region with authority to do whatever was necessary to run this most notorious of badmen to earth. Major McCullough realized it was a political move on the governor's part, the signal corpsman told us confidentially, but it was still a slap in the army's face — almost telling them that they couldn't do their job and needed outside help.

We turned our horses and mules in with the stage company stock in the adobe-walled corral, and the three of us turned in early and slept soundly on cots in the small station, The dour-faced man who ran the station and his young assistant had their own rooms adjoining the main room of the station.

After a heavy breakfast the next morning, we paid our bill, hitched up, repacked, and pushed on toward Fort Bowie. We were traveling back over this same road less than two weeks after we had been here before, but it seemed like a different place. The arroyos and desert washes appeared as dry as if it hadn't rained in forty years. The only thing that gave the lie to this was the water of the big, normally dry playa shimmering in the morning sun off to our right as we traveled east near the base of the Dos Cabezas Mountains.

When we pulled off the stage road to pay a visit to the Dos Cabezas camp, I saw no activity on the side of the mountain. The side road dipped into a wash. As we came up the other side a few minutes later, I caught sight of the camp in the distance, but still saw no one. As we crossed the dry ford and started the last few hundred yards, the camp appeared deserted.

"Where is everybody?" Wiley asked, voicing all our thoughts.

Burke reined up the mules in the middle of the tent and shack camp at the foot of the slope. No one showed. Nothing stirred. The warm autumn sunshine beat down on us, and the silence settled in as we halted and looked around. A fitful, light breeze brushed the desert mesquite. It was eerie — almost like a ghost town.

"Wonder if the ore ran out suddenly?" Burke said.

"If so, they took off in a hurry. They left some of their wagons and tents," I answered.

"Hey!" came a faint cry. "Hey!" A tent flap

was thrown back and a man hobbled out, leaning on a makeshift crutch. "You were the men who were here a few weeks ago," he said, limping toward us. His left pants leg was ripped up above the knee and his leg was heavily bandaged. "You're probably wonderin' where everybody is." He grinned, squinting up at us in the sun, obviously relishing the look of bewilderment on our faces.

"Yes."

"Well, sir, I'll tell ya. About a dozen of them lit out after Mad Dog and one of his boys. I'd be with 'em, 'cept I broke my leg in a fall a couple days ago."

"Mad Dog?" I was incredulous. "He's down by the Mexican border somewhere."

"Not according to that Mexican who was riding with him," the man replied, still savoring our confusion.

"What's going on, Mr. . . . ?" Wiley demanded, getting impatient.

"Couch. Charley Couch's the name. What Mexican? Why, that one laid out like a log over there in the wagon. Told us his name was Jacinto Cruz. Couple of the boys found him near the road early this morning. He died of an old, mortified leg wound about an hour later. When the boys brought him into camp, he told us he and another outlaw and Mad Dog had been torturing that old hermit, Crozier, all night, tryin' to get him to tell them where his gold was hid and . . ."

247

"Wait a minute," Burke interrupted. "What gold?"

"Well, Mad Dog somehow got the idea that the old drunk had a secret stash of gold somewhere. The rumor got out that he was the one who was secretly dropping off those pokes of gold for people who were hurt or in trouble. Anyway, from what this Mexican said, the three of them caught Crozier, drunk as usual, last night in a little cabin just west of here and worked him over pretty good trying to make him tell where his gold was. Guess he finally broke down and told them, after they'd tortured him might near to death. Anyway, Mad Dog left Crozier and headed straight off east toward Apache Pass just after daylight."

"What about Cruz?"

"He told us Mad Dog just left him behind because his wound had poisoned him and got so much worse he couldn't ride. That was one mad Mexican! Whew! He was close t'dyin' when they brought him in, but he'd a'put a knife in that Mad Dog if he coulda got his hands on him. He said Mad Dog just tossed him a bottle of Crozier's brandy and told him to have a last drink before he cashed in, then just laughed and rode off, leavin' him there. Musta been hate that gave him the strength to crawl almost to the stage road where the boys found him."

He turned and hobbled over to the tongue of a parked buckboard and eased himself down. "Whew! Gotta get the weight off this leg.

248

Anyhow, as I was sayin', when the boys heard the tale this greaser told us, they were furious. There was a big hoorah to go after them . . .''

"Hell, are you telling us that the men in this camp suddenly got brave?" Burke snorted. "Is this the same bunch of miners who wouldn't go after Mad Dog the night he kicked in Shorty Anderson's ribs? I can't believe it!"

"Maybe they're after the reward," Wiley put in.

"Oh, yes, we heard about that reward," Couch said. "It only pays if he's brought in alive to stand trial. But as riled up as those boys were when they took outa here, I wouldn't bet on anybody collectin' a reward — *if* they catch up to him."

"Did Crozier actually admit having some gold?" I asked. "Where?"

Couch shrugged. "The Mex said Crozier told 'em about an old, abandoned mine in Apache Pass he'd been takin' almost pure gold out of."

Burke and I looked at each other. That had to be the old mine in which we'd spent the night!

"Hell, a man will say anything — true or not — if he's tortured enough," Wiley grunted.

"Still can't figure this bunch of miners suddenly getting all worked up because some drunk got beat up," Wiley said. "Maybe they're just stampeding after Crozier's gold themselves."

"Don't think so," Charley Couch replied. "The boys were just fed up, mostly. Charlie Singleton, Bob Welch, Vance Leary, Jack

Scruggs, even old cool-headed Bill Hawkins. This was the last straw. We heard about that shootin' and robbin' over at the San Pedro stage station. And I think the boys just figgered we'd never be rid of the danger unless we did sumthin' ourselves. And this was the time to do it, what with Mad Dog not expectin' it and all. Besides, his gang had been whittled down to just him and one other man. Crozier's a pitiful specimen of a man, but he *is* a kindly fella. Never hurt nobody but himself. He's sure well liked by everybody here."

"Yeah, I know," I nodded. "He saved our lives a few weeks back."

"Three of the men in a buckboard went over to see if he's still alive after that beating and torture," Couch said. "They should be back here 'most any time. About a dozen o' the rest rode off hell-bent toward Apache Pass about an hour ago to see if they could catch up with Mad Dog and his partner."

I had dismounted, ground-reining my horse as Couch talked. I sidled over to the wagon he had indicated earlier, and looked over the tailboard. A scrap of brown canvas covered something in the wagon bed. I flipped back the corner of the cover and found myself staring into the upside-down face of Jacinto Cruz. I touched his throat. He was dead, all right — apparently of the improperly treated leg wound Burke had given him that night in the rocks. As I flipped the cover back in place, Burke was out of the wagon and throwing a saddle blanket on the spare Morgan.

"Where are you going?"

"After them," he replied shortly, heaving the saddle into place and reaching for the cinch.

"One of you boys got a smoke?" Couch asked.

Wiley fished absently in his pocket and threw him his tobacco pouch from the wagon seat.

"Why don't you stay here and see if you can help in case they bring Crozier in alive?" I suggested to Wiley as I remounted. Burke was already in the saddle and yanking loose the reins of the pack horse from the back of the wagon. Burke pulled his horse's head around and kicked him into motion, pulling the pack horse after him. I sensed that Wiley was exasperated at being left behind, but I didn't look back or give him a chance to say anything, as I spurred my Arabian after Burke.

I had no idea what kind of horseman the small, wiry, Irish New Yorker was, but I soon found out. Even though he led the pack horse that held his portable photographic outfit, I found it a real job to keep up with him. My Arabian gelding, Samson, had already carried me at a walk about forty miles this day, but he responded gallantly for the first mile or two, stretching out into a long gallop once we hit the stage road. The tall horse had such a smooth stride that I felt as if I were astride a gently rocking hard leather chair, instead of the army-issue McClellan. It was a gallant effort, but after about two miles, I felt him begin to falter and eased him back and gradually slowed him to a walk. Whatever it was we were chasing, I felt it wasn't worth killing a very game horse to catch. The men from Dos Cabezas had more than an hour's head start, and Mad Dog had two or three times that, I guessed. Burke continued to pull away from me, without looking back. It seemed as if he sensed that a showdown was imminent, and he, as the photographer, had to be there to record it. I wondered how the Morgans had the stamina to keep up the pace Burke was setting for them. I had always thought of Morgans as good for the shorter distances, but not necessarily the longer. The pack horse, especially, had carried a pack over forty miles today, even though it wasn't a heavy one.

As Burke gradually disappeared in the mesquite and sage ahead of me, I got off and walked, leading my winded horse. I could keep track of his progress by a faint cloud of dust rising over him. The dust cloud seemed to slow, and then disappeared. He had either slowed to a walk himself, I reflected, or had entered Apache Pass and was out of view.

Just then I noticed my horse had a perceptible limp. Possibly a stone bruise, I thought. But I stopped and pulled up his left forefoot for a look. He had picked up a small stone, which I carefully wedged out with my knife. I continued to walk him, however, for some time, even though the limp had disappeared.

Another thirty minutes brought me close to the break in the mountain ranges that was the beginning of Apache Pass. Samson followed the empty stage road with no hesitation, walking steadily. He gave no indication that he sensed any danger that I could neither see nor hear. But the ominous desert silence oppressed me. How far ahead was Burke? What had he found, if anything? A south wind had begun to blow, whisking away any sound from the direction of the pass. Even thought I heard no shots, I had the same empty feeling as when Wiley and I had ridden into the pass from the other end several weeks before.

I was all eyes and ears as I slowly entered the pass, the road dipping and then rising to the summit of the pass. Then the road took a long winding descent before leveling off in the area where we had fought the Apaches. The mine entrance where Crozier had saved us was a black square against the hillside a few hundred yards to my right. Not a living thing was in sight. A strange rushing sound forced itself on my consciousness. I looked around and finally identified it as the wind rushing through a thick stand of century plants on the hillside above me. The wind was still blowing hard up above, but I was in the calm of the protected area below it.

Instinctively, I rode toward the mine entrance, my Colt in my hand. But nothing was there. I dismounted, tied Samson to an outcropping of rock, and stepped inside. After my eyes accustomed themselves to the dimness, I walked back into the tunnel until the light from the entrance failed to penetrate and I had to feel my way along, as I had done once before. Just as I was on the point of turning back, I made out some light ahead, and went on until I stood in the small room where we had kept our horses the night that already seemed so long ago. A shaft of midday sunlight lighted the room from the surface of the hilltop about a hundred feet above me. The room contained nothing and showed no evidence of any recent mining. If Crozier was taking gold out of here, it must be somewhere deeper in the mine. Two timbered tunnels ran off deeper into the hill at slight angles to each other, but I had no time and no light to do any exploring now. I felt my way back to the entrance. I was not good enough at reading the signs to tell if anyone had been at the mine in the past few hours. The ground bore some scuff marks and partial hoofprints, and the rocks near the entrance were scratched with marks which might have been made by shod hooves. But these could have been made by anything, even Crozier's mule.

I remounted and continued following the old stage road as it wound down gradually into the broadening pass. I knew the stage station was coming up soon, and approached cautiously, stopping my horse as soon as the stone building came in sight. Nothing appeared unusual. In fact, nothing appeared at all. The place was quiet. Precisely because I didn't want to go into any long explanations, I gave the station a wide berth so as to remain out of sight. If Mad Dog or the men from Dos Cabezas or Burke had stopped here, they had moved on. No extra horses were anywhere in sight. I wanted to find them before I saw anyone else. But I had to admit, for all I knew, Mad Dog might have gone straight on through into the New Mexico Territory on the other side, after he found out that Crozier had lied about gold in the old mine. Hawkins and the Dos Cabezas men might be miles ahead on his trail, with Burke bringing up the rear a mile or two ahead of me. I let my horse have his head until we reached the point about two hundred yards farther where the stage road joined the broad, sandy wash that was Siphon Canyon, and turned left to follow the winding course of the canyon almost to the eastern terminus of the pass.

I pulled up my horse and sat listening to the silence. Even the wind was blowing so far above me now that I could no longer hear it. Should I continue following the stage road down the canyon and out the other side, or should I ride up the canyon and connect with the military road to Fort Bowie? Maybe if I got up higher on one of the surrounding ridges, I could at least see some dust in the distance. Siphon Canyon, where I sat my horse, besides being used as the stagecoach road to traverse about half of Apache Pass, was one of the main routes for rainwater runoff from the surrounding mountains. As such, it had long since become thickly coated with deep sand. The prevalence of water guaranteed a dense growth of large mesquite on both sides of the sandy wash and, more unusual for this desert terrain, many large cottonwood, oak, and walnut trees also lined this narrow canyon, sinking their roots deep to the subsurface water. The boles of some of these trees were several feet around near the base.

While I was still trying to make up my mind which way to go, I heard the muffled sound of hoofbeats coming down the canyon toward me. I quickly eased my horse back into the dense thickets to await the coming of the horsemen, whoever they might be. The hoofbeats were coming closer at a gallop. They swept into sight around a bend and thundered within a few yards of me as they turned into the stage road heading west. From the thick brush of my hiding place I caught glimpses of Hawkins's white hair under his hat and several other men who looked familiar. There were at least ten riders, apparently all of the men from Dos Cabezas. As soon as the riders were past me and out of sight, I kneed my horse out of the mesquite and kicked him into a lope up Siphon Canyon.

I had probably gone a little more than half a mile when I came around a tight turn and pulled Samson to a sliding halt in the sand. Cold chills went up my back at the sight before me. In the middle of the wash stood a huge walnut tree with overhanging limbs. Directly in front of me at eye level hung the dead bodies of Mad Dog and the short outlaw named Billy!

My horse shied at the sudden sight or smell of this apparition and danced around in a half-circle before I could rein him back and take another look at the double hanging. The hands were tied behind them and they were hatless. Billy's eyes were shut, but Mad Dog's were partly open, staring glazedly at nothing. Their heads were cocked grotesquely to one side and their mouths, in the swollen, unshaven faces, were slightly open, as if gasping for one last breath. The tail ends of the ropes that passed over the thick limb were secured to the base of the big walnut tree.

All the details of this scene impressed themselves on me in a matter of seconds. I was shocked. I don't know what I had expected to find, but this wasn't it. I guess the men of Dos Cabezas had not impressed me as man-hunters. Or else the awesome reputation of Mad Dog had somehow made him seem invincible in my imagination. A deadly fascination held me. I couldn't draw my gaze away from the dangling bodies still turning slowly in their hemp collars.

"Matt!"

I jumped, and the hair stood up on the back of my neck. I jerked around toward the voice, reaching for my gun. No one.

"Matt! Over here!"

Burke pushed his way out into the wash from the thick screen of mesquite a few yards to my right.

"Where the hell did you come from?" I was confused as I reholstered my Colt. "Where's your horse?"

"Helluva sight, isn't it?" He jerked his thumb toward the dangling bodies. "C'mon. I've gotta get these plates into my dark tent and develop them." He disappeared into the foliage.

I dismounted and walked up a few yards until I found a break in the dense growth barely wide enough to lead my horse out of the wash. Burke had already removed the plate and holder from his stereoscopic camera on the tripod in the bushes and was just squeezing into his small dark tent about fifty yards back, near a willow tree. His horse and pack horse were tied another twenty or thirty yards farther away in a clump of mesquite. I tied my horse to a bush, my mind in a whirl. But I contented myself with making a quick inspection tour of the surrounding area to be sure no one else was hiding close by. We were no more than a mile from Fort Bowie, but completely screened off from it by the rugged cut-up terrain and thick growth and big trees along the canyon bottoms. Unless a patrol happened by, we were as out of touch with the military as if we had been on the other side of the mountains.

In a few minutes Burke emerged from the dark tent into the shade of the willow tree, and held up the dripping plate so both of us could see. The twin negative images were sharp and vivid. I gasped at what the clear light revealed. The sharply etched figures of the two hanging outlaws were in the center. Grouped around them were the mounted figures of the men who had just passed me on the trail, nearly every one of them recognizable. There were Charley Singleton and Bob Welch, the tall and short partners who had first greeted us at Dos Cabezas. There were some others whose faces were familiar, and a couple who were apparently newcomers. And sitting on his horse at the left of the picture was Bill Hawkins. It was as dramatic a scene as I had ever beheld, and it had taken place no more than a half-hour before, only a few yards away. Now the event was frozen in time, an immutable record of the execution of two of the most notorious criminals in the southwest.

"How the hell did you catch up with them," I asked, as Burke took the plate and held it out by the edges for the sun to dry.

"When I caught sight of them, they had just flushed Mad Dog and his man out of the mine," the redhead replied. "I was a good ways off and no one saw me. They were too busy to look my way, anyhow. But I just kept out of sight until they got Mad Dog and Billy on their horses with their hands tied, and then followed at a good distance. When they headed on into the pass, I thought they were going to turn them over to the military at Fort Bowie. But when they stopped in the canyon, I couldn't really figure out what they were up to because they were screened off by all the brush and trees." Still holding the plate by the edges, he turned it over for the sun to hit the other side. "Anyway," he continued, "when I finally suspected what they were about, I had to really scramble to get my gear off the pack horse and get up close with it. Had to treat that collodian plate in the dark tent there under the willow and then hurry to get the stereoscopic camera set up without being seen. Whew! Now *that* was some trick! If they hadn't been so intent on what they were doing, and if it hadn't been for this thick growth along the canyon bottom, I never could have done it. Even when I squirmed in there with the camera and tripod and got set up where I could see, I had to guess at the exposure because of the sunlight and shadow. They had just whipped the horses from under the pair o' them as I was getting set up, so there was plenty of noise and commotion to cover any little movement I was making in the thick bushes." He shook his head in disbelief, looking again at the plate he held in his hands as if it were solid gold. "What luck! I caught them just at the right time. There wasn't much movement and everyone was just staring at the pair of them." He couldn't conceal his excitement. "This is it! This is the shot I've been looking for. This is the view that's going to make me famous!"

Chapter 17

"Marshal Cameron is madder than a nest of wasps," Wiley grinned at me two days later as he came out of the adjutant's office at Fort Bowie. He jerked a thumb over his shoulder. "He's raising hell in there with the major."

"What about?"

"He thinks the troops should have prevented that lynching of Mad Dog and his man in Siphon Canyon, since it happened not over a mile from here. The major's getting pretty red in the face. He'll probably throw Cameron out of the office in a minute."

"I hear he's ready to arrest anyone who had anything to do with that hanging."

"Right. But the problem is, even though it's generally known who did it, nobody is talking. He has no proof, and nobody is admitting to knowing anything."

"This is a politically explosive issue," I said. "I'm sure the marshal is dreading going back to face Governor Hoyt. That hanging was exactly what he didn't want to happen. If Mad Dog and Billy had been gunned down in a robbery attempt or escape attempt, it wouldn't have been so bad. But they were captured and should have been turned over to the law."

"Yeah, and it wasn't like those miners didn't know about the reward and the governor wanting them alive."

"I'd guess Hawkins had a lot to do with convincing the miners to hang them," I said. "And I think I know why. There've been so many killers tried and turned loose by slick lawyers in Tucson in the past few years that he convinced the miners the same thing would happen to Mad Dog and Billy. Those outlaws had enough gold to buy the best, and crookedest, attorneys and jury."

"Could those Dos Cabezas miners really be prosecuted?" Wiley asked, falling in beside me as we walked toward the mess hall in the late-afternoon sun. "After all, this is a wild frontier territory. Hell, there's no way they could actually convict these men of murder for defending themselves against outlaws and killers, is there?"

I shrugged. "Don't know. According to the marshal, the governor was going to make a showcase trial out of Mad Dog. He wanted the world to see that orderly justice was possible in the Arizona Territory. It sure would have helped the argument for statehood and for attracting permanent settlers."

"Yeah." Wiley grinned again. "This is going to make the governor look like a fool after all that publicity. If he's irritated enough over this, I guess he might make an example of that lynch crowd by putting them on trial for taking the law into their own hands."

"He's apparently determined to have law and

order at any price, according to the marshal."

We paused outside the mess hall to allow a group of soldiers to go inside ahead of us. "What about the picture Burke took?" Wiley asked, glancing around and lowering his voice. "There won't be any doubt about the identity of those men when that gets out."

"I know," I nodded. "Burke says this is the view that will make his reputation. He plans to sell thousands of them on stereopticon viewer cards. He's been over in the wagon printing them up ever since we got here." I glanced down the slope behind the sutler's store where Burke's converted ambulance was parked. "In fact, I think I'll walk down there before I go to supper and have a little talk with him."

"Think you can persuade him not to publish that photograph?"

"I can try. I can't see those men being arrested for what they did."

"But Burke has been looking for this one big picture for a long time. If he's right about this view making him famous, he might never have another chance." Wiley shook his head. "I'd sure hate to have that choice."

"We talked about it earlier, and I'm sure it's on his mind. But he made no mention about suppressing the picture. Think I'll amble down there and try one last time. You want to go?"

"You might do better by yourself," Wiley suggested. "He seems to listen more to what you say."

"Okay. I'll see you after supper."

I was sitting cross-legged on the ground when Burke opened the back door of his wagon to expose the plate and treated paper to the sun to make another print. He nodded to me, but went about his business without speaking. As soon as the print was exposed for a second, he covered it and climbed back into the wagon, handing it to his apprentice, who was working inside. "That's it for today, Chris. The sun is too far gone to make good prints now. Go ahead and finish that one, and we'll pick it up tomorrow."

He closed the door and came over to me, "You about ready to eat?"

"Sure am. Wiley's already up at the mess hall." I changed the subject. "I see you got another pair of mules today."

"Yeah. I decided I could afford it. The major had two good ones to spare. He wanted a steep price for them, with harness, but I met his price. My money worries should be over soon."

"So you're going to go ahead and publish it?"

"Sure. Why not? This is it. My ticket to fame and fortune."

"You know that's all the evidence the marshal needs to arrest those miners — and probably get a conviction, too."

"Hell. I didn't hang those men; I just took the picture." He sounded exasperated.

I remained silent for a few minutes, picking up small stones from between my crossed legs and tossing them away, trying to appear casual. The

264

setting sun was painting deep purple hollows on the rugged mountain slopes west of the fort.

"Those miners did everybody a favor," I finally said. "Do you think they deserve to go to jail?"

"I'm not getting into the morality of it," he shot back. "Like I said, I just took the picture."

"Yes, but the picture was more important than bringing those outlaws in for a fair trail. You didn't try to prevent the miners from hanging them." I knew I was pushing, but I felt I had to get him to face the issue and his decision, squarely.

"Look," he said, turning to me as if this were his last word on the matter, "I got there too late to prevent it. Even if I had ridden straight on and caught up to them before the hanging, there was nothing I could have done to prevent it, judging from the mood that crowd was in. Besides, you know yourself that those two killers would probably have been hanged if they had been brought in alive and tried. It's not my job to decide the guilt or innocence of the executioners."

"Maybe not, but you'll be deciding their fate if you publish that picture. As long as you didn't do anything to prevent their actions, why see to it that they are arrested for it? You claim to be neutral. If they are guilty of killing by that lynching, then why not let the Almighty punish them, instead of a human court?"

"Then why have human courts at all?" he retorted. "Besides, no court would convict them once the facts are known."

"You have no assurance of that. Governor Hoyt is hopping mad. I heard he sent a blistering telegram to Marshal Cameron this afternoon demanding the arrest of all those involved. And you know political pressure. It'll overwhelm justice and reason nearly every time."

Burke turned away from me, his mouth a grim line. He went over and leaned his hand on a rear wagon wheel, staring off toward the west. He was silent for a long time as I continued to sit cross-legged on the ground. The sun slid farther down the sky until it was a brilliant fireball resting on the jagged horizon.

The back door of the wagon opened and Chris climbed down, wiping his hands on a towel he then tossed back inside. "Finished. Whew! I'm tired. It's good to get back to work at something I like, but I'm still weak. The doc let me do a few things around the post, but I'm going to have to work myself back into shape." The blond youth rolled down his sleeves and buttoned them against the cool evening breeze that was beginning to sweep across the pass. He looked at me and then at Burke's back where he still stood by the corner of the wagon, and apparently sensed something was wrong. "I'm hungry. Anybody want to go eat?"

From behind me, inside the quadrangle of the fort, the clear notes of the bugler sounding "retreat" began, as a detail lowered the flag in the middle of the parade ground.

Suddenly Burke spun on his heel, jerked open the back door of the wagon, and climbed inside. A few seconds later he reappeared with a glass negative plate in his hands. He climbed down and strode over to a large boulder nearby. With no hesitation he flung the plate against it, shattering the glass into fragments. Then he ground the larger shards into small pieces with his boot-heel, seeming to vent his frustration and anger.

"There, dammit. That ought to settle the issue once and for all. I hope you're satisfied now."

With that he stalked off toward the mess hall, and Chris, after looking accusingly at me, followed him.

There was an empty feeling in the pit of my stomach as I watched them go. I got slowly to my feet and looked back where the last rays of the setting sun were reflected on the smashed pieces of glass. They were the only physical remnants of a shattered dream — a dream of many years that had finally been realized, only to be destroyed for the sake of protecting a group of virtual strangers.

I had won my argument, but somehow I felt like the loser.

Chapter 18

The next morning we packed our gear and were about ready to say our good-bye's to Dr. Donnelly and Major McCullough and leave. Burke was not very talkative, but I could hardly blame him. I felt uneasy, thinking that Burke was probably blaming me for the loss of his dream. After all we had been through together, I hated to part on a sour note.

The Irishman indicated that he and Chris might head east out of the pass to check on some of the recent silver strikes in the southwestern mountains of the New Mexico Territory. Wiley and I had discussed retracing our steps as far as the San Pedro stage station and then turning south to look at the new Tombstone claim where rich silver was being discovered, just a few miles east of the new Fort Huachuca.

"You'll never guess what I just heard," Chris said as he came up to the wagon, his eyes shining with excitement.

"And what might that be?" Wiley asked, stowing a small sack of cornmeal in the pack he was making up.

"I was just over at the hospital saying good-bye to Dr. Donnelly, and then I went in to ask how that Crozier fella was doing. He's got some broken ribs and is pretty beat up, but I got to talking to him about how good a man the doc was and how they'd take good care of him and all. Well, he slipped me this gold nugget he had stuck down in his mattress. Told me it was to help me get established."

He fished in his pocket and pulled out a nugget as big as the end of my thumb. Some slight tracings of quartz ran through it, but it appeared to be nearly pure. It was an irregular shape, but smooth, as if worn by water action. I whistled softly. "Very nice."

"But that's not all," the apprentice continued. "He told me he was the one who threw that poke of gold dust through the major's window for that bartender, Shorty Anderson, who was here until last week. I got to asking him about that gold you said was left at the stage station for the family of that man Mad Dog shot and threw into the river. He told me about some others, too. He's been scattering gold all over the place for people who are having bad luck. Said he's been sending it right along to his wife and family back in Tennessee, too."

"Where's he getting it?" Burke asked.

"He said it was no secret now. It's out of that old mine down here in Apache Pass. He said everybody thought it was played out. Not so. A long time ago the Apaches killed the men who were working it, and it was abandoned. When whites came in later they didn't find anything in it, so they thought it had been worked out. But he explored all its tunnels. He was digging around in one that had been partly caved in, and found a really rich vein. As soon as he could get to Tucson on his mule, he had it registered as his claim and has been working it for over a year."

"And everybody thought he was just a common drunk," I said.

"Instead of a rich drunk," Wiley finished.

"He may drink too much for his own good, but he's certainly not as crazy as he acts," Paddy Burke said. "Crazy like a fox."

"A rich Good Samaritan in the guise of a smelly derelict. Damn!" Wiley shook his head. "You just never know . . ."

"Doc says he'll heal up all right, providing he hasn't missed any internal injuries. But it's going to take a while," Chris continued. "Mr. Crozier tried to bribe me to sneak a bottle of brandy to him. I told him Doc Donnelly said he couldn't have any. But Mr. Crozier said I was a good boy and to keep the nugget anyway. Told me I deserved it for getting sliced up by those Apaches."

"Is that scar still pretty sensitive?" I asked.

"Just when I bump it certain ways. Doc says some nerves were cut, and it will probably always be a little sensitive."

"Wait 'til your friends back home get a look at that," Burke said. "You're probably one of the few people who's ever been cut at close range by an Apache warrior and lived to tell about it."

"Yeah. They'll never believe it. I'll have some tales to tell. Some of the pictures we've been taking may make them believe that it really happened." He grinned.

"Have you decided where you're going from here?" I asked Burke.

"Probably east into the New Mexico Territory," he said, shutting the back door of the wagon.

"Still looking for that one great photograph?"

"No. I've already got it." He grinned slyly, turning to face me.

"What?"

"That's right. That plate I broke last night was another view I took of the hanging a few seconds earlier. It wasn't much good — blurred from the movement."

"Well, I'll be damned! And I was almost feeling sorry for you."

"As a matter of fact, I came that close to destroying the good plate. But I just couldn't do it. I'd worked too hard and been too lucky to get it. Besides," he grinned, "it would have been cheating history." He put up his hand as I started to object. "Don't worry. I won't publish that picture until this blows over. I don't expect the turmoil to last but a few months at the most. In any case, I won't release it until there's little or no danger to those men. And then I'll release it back east where the biggest market is. There will be no names with the picture, except the names of the outlaws. Photographs can't be reproduced, so it will be a long shot that someone will recognize anyone in that picture. Anyway, I

271

don't think anyone will care by then. Some of those men will be gone. The political scene moves on. Who knows what territorial governor may be in power by then?"

I nodded, accepting his logic. I felt a great sense of relief, as if a load had been lifted from my shoulders. It was the best solution any of us could have wanted. The picture was intact, and Burke's future was secure. And the miners who had disposed of Mad Dog would be in little danger of exposure and prosecution.

"I'd be glad for you and Wiley to travel with us," Burke continued. "Never know what we'll run into over in those new digs."

"Thanks, but Wiley and I are going to take a look at those new Tombstone claims before we head to Tucson. Maybe we'll go to Prescott, or on over to California. We haven't really decided for sure. One thing I do know — I have to get busy and finish my series of articles for *Harper's Weekly*. Too bad I can't give all the details of that hanging and your part in recording it. But I'll tell as much as I can."

"It'll whet their appetites." Burke laughed. "Always leave your readers begging for more."

I smiled with satisfaction as I looked through a notch in Apache Pass toward the blue haze in the distance. The haze hid not only the distant land, but also the dangers ahead.